D. M. Thomas is the author of five books of verse, the most recent being *The Honeymoon Voyage* (1978), in which year he won a Cholmondeley Award for poetry; his children's book, *The Devil and the Floral Dance*, also appeared in 1978. Born in Cornwall in 1935, Thomas was educated at New College, Oxford, and learnt Russian while doing his national service. He has published two volumes of translations of the poems of Anna Akhmatova, *Requiem* and *Poem without a Hero* (1976) and *Way of All the Earth* (selected poems, 1979), and after fifteen years as a lecturer at the Hereford College of Education, went back to Oxford in 1978 to do research in problems of verse translation. *The Flute-Player* is his first novel.

D. M. Thomas

The Flute-Player

published by Pan Books PICADOR

First published 1979 by Victor Gollancz Ltd
This Picador edition published 1980 by Pan Books Ltd,
Cavaye Place, London SW10 9PG
© D. M. Thomas 1979
ISBN 0 330 26027 8
Set, printed and bound in Great Britain by
Cox & Wyman Ltd, Reading

to the memory of

Anna Akhmatova, Osip Mandelstam,
Boris Pasternak, and Marina Tsvetaeva

('There are Four of Us')

Quotations ascribed in this novel to two
of the fictional characters are from:

Akhmadulina, Akhmatova, Baudelaire, Chapman,
Dante, Emily Dickinson, Eliot, Frost, Lorca, Mandelstam,
Nadezhda Mandelstam, Pasternak, Sylvia Plath, Pushkin, Rilke,
Anne Sexton, Shakespeare, Gaspara Stampa, Tsvetaeva, and
Yeats. May they forgive the author for these misappropriations
and distortions.

D.M.T.

Chapter One

The light switch did not work. The grumbling old janitor had had to be woken up to turn on the water and the heating; she dare not disturb him again. It was still cold; she kept her coat on. She looked around the bleak room, filling with dusk, and could not imagine it ever seeming like home. Yet she was glad of shelter, glad to be alive. She was hungry, and ate one of the apples she had bought at the stall, and a piece of bread.

There was a tune going round her head and she was annoyed because she could not place it.

The girl lay in bed listening to the quarrel in the room next to hers. The argument of the man and the woman got louder, she could hear occasional scuffles. It was hard to tell whether the creaking of their bed was lovemaking or murder. Was that the cry of a woman's orgasm or a knife in the breast? She lay wide-eyed, imagining. The baby had been crying for hours, with neither of them bothering to comfort the poor lamb. She thought of ringing the police; but in these times there was no one to bother himself with such trivialities as a baby crying for hours, cold or hungry or wet.

The noises settled, and she tried to sleep. She started to pray, but the maddening tune came back, interrupting her prayer and carrying her into sleep.

She was jolted awake by a man's scream, so near it might have been the same pillow. The girl's heart pounded. The baby started howling, she heard a door slam and rapid feet pass with the crying baby and hurry with it downstairs. There was silence for a time, and she began to wonder if she had dreamt it. Then she heard an engine, a siren. It stopped outside. Heavy feet ran up the stairs. A short while later, through a window so grimy it hardly separated night from dawn, she saw the ambulance men manoeuvring a stretcher into the ambulance.

A week later there was a knock on her door. She opened it to a bearded young man. He was her next-door neighbour, he said, and wondered if she had seen or heard anything of his wife and child. She invited him in. He looked ill, and she made him rest on the sofa while she boiled the kettle for some tea. No, she had seen and heard nothing of them since the night when he had been taken away by ambulance. He sighed and looked as though he might burst into tears. Over the tea he told her all about it. He seemed relieved to get it off his chest, and she was a patient listener because she was naturally curious.

He and his wife had known each other since childhood, he said, and in fact came from the same family. This was probably the root of the problem. She was neurotically intent on proving how equal she was. If he didn't do his fair share with the housework and looking after the baby, there were ructions.

Quarrels even arose — and this he did not admit before much stumbling and prompting — over their intimate life. Normal intercourse (for he was no pervert) now struck his wife as an invasion. They had had terrible rows over this, and it ought to have warned him she was cracking up. The girl gave him more tea, and made it clear he need not be afraid to mention such intimacies. She knew about life. She was not squeamish. She had heard the groanings of their bed, and been disturbed. He apologized and was embarrassed. No need to be, she said; they couldn't help it if the walls were thin.

The girl suggested that some women became acutely depressed after childbirth. The man shook his head. They had been quarrelling for much longer than that; his wife had really never wanted a baby.

He could hardly speak of it without blushing. He had asserted his manhood, letting the baby cry till she had been forced to go and change him. Then they had had another fierce row in bed — she had probably heard some of it — but his wife had seemed to calm down eventually. She had been unresponsive to his lovemaking but no more than usual. He had been woken up by a dreadful pain. His thighs were wet and warm, at first he thought something had happened to his bladder, but then he realized it was much worse, he was bleeding profusely from his penis. She had let him sleep, and then drawn out his foreskin and bitten it off — literally bitten it off, or as good as: in the hospital (if one could call it hospital in these days) they had done a rush circumcision to prevent septic poisoning and even more drastic surgery.

In this house, where nobody would answer a cry for help, he might easily have bled to death. He had staggered to the phone down the corridor, and by a miracle it was working. Of course if he had known someone had moved in next door . . .

The young man was shaking, and the girl took his hand. She felt sorry for him but also troubled by an irrepressible urge to smile. It might be all for the best, she told him. Wasn't circumcision healthier, supposedly, and wasn't it meant to be better for your sex life? – accompanying this encouragement with a beautiful broad grin. As for his wife, it sounded as if he was better off without her. He must trust she would take care of the baby till they could be traced.

He was touched by her kindness. They talked all evening, about marriages, broken homes, the violent times they lived in, and they got on so well together it seemed only natural for him to fall asleep in her bed, rather than face too soon the unpleasant associations of his own. In the morning she gave him tea again; and unwound the bandage from his penis and bathed it gently and rubbed ointment on. He flinched, but bore up bravely. He moved his few things into her room where she could look after him while he recovered. Rents were high in the city, and people were always crowding together.

He confessed he was worried whether it would prove possible for him to enjoy sex again. A few days after he had moved in she persuaded him to try. Very gently she stroked his penis into erection, making sure she did not touch the foreskin or glans, and tenderly she helped him ease it into her vagina. She lay quietly and taught him to enjoy an absolute stillness within her, for twenty minutes, while she maintained his erection with kisses and nibbles at his throat and ear-lobes, and delicate strokings of his thighs and scrotum. Her body lay at rest under him. He withdrew without coming. And the next time, she suggested he just try gently moving in and out when his prick was so tumid with blood and desire it scarcely belonged to him, and he managed this, and came into her without too much pain. He cried with joy and she cradled him like a baby. He was happy, and gradually, so gradually, day by day and night by night, she guided his recovery, till he was able to fuck her hard, and bring her off; but she was careful never to trouble him by climbing on top, or being too aggressive. Except, occasionally, he *wanted* her to bite him, or climb on top. And then he would look in the mirror and see two little love-bites in his throat, as though a serpent without poison had visited him in his sleep, and he would smile.

Chapter Two

No news came of the man's wife and child, nor did he expect any. When you vanished, it was usually for ever. What worried them especially was that she had left their ration books on the dresser: tantamount to a declaration of non-existence. They were painfully aware that the child's misfortune was allowing them to eat reasonably for a while. Then the police came, had a look around, and took away the extra ration books. They suspected they had upset the janitor in some way – maybe the soldiers who had moved in next door had overheard their conversation and maliciously reported it. Or maybe the room was bugged: you could never be sure of anything. In these times the janitor was father, mother, sister, lover and boss. All went in fear and trembling of him. It was rumoured that the old man upstairs, janitor of the big apartment block in which they lived, had been butler in the former palace. Some said he had been the rich owner himself. If so he probably carried even more authority than usual. The man and the girl were always very careful to say 'Good morning' or 'Good evening' to him, on the rare occasions when they passed him on the stairs or landing. At first he had been amiable enough in his morose way; but lately it was clear they had offended him. He stared at the girl with particular malevolence.

The man went out every morning and returned at dusk. No one, in these times, asked what you were doing or even where you came from. He was secretive even with her – and that suited her well, because she was still waiting for the meaning of her life to unroll; it was a secret even from herself. The two of them fitted together rather nicely, and they decided to get married. A simple declaration was sufficient. There were no church marriages nor registry offices. One seized what happiness one could. The girl, for example, got a lot of pleasure just watching the maple tree growing outside the window. Once, in winter, the pipes burst and the room was flooded. The electricity had gone; he went to light an oil lamp. When he returned, its yellow light caught her figure, dressed only in a short plain nightdress, stooping and rising with a large earthenware bowl brimming with water. The muscles of her face and neck were tensed with the weight, her sad eyes were concentrated on her task, her cheeks and forehead glistened, her breasts, half exposed, heaved slightly. He stood turned to stone with the lantern, realizing her beauty for the first time.

When they started cleaning up the wreckage left by the flood, they thought they would make the room more cheerful. She was good with the sewing machine he had – very optimistically – given to his first wife. Even some cheap blue curtains made all the difference, she thought: curtains and some bright wallpaper. In one respect they were in luck: a part of the house had been allocated to artists and writers; they had made friends with some of them and managed to scrounge a few unwanted paintings and carvings to put around their room. The furniture and fittings were basic; and what could you do with the ugly green bath and toilet in the corner except keep the screen in place? But at least the room began to look more lived-in and homely.

The girl – Elena – earned a few shillings posing for one of the sculptors from the artists' colony. A strong, barrel-chested young man, he carved his sculpture closer to his vision while cooking a shish kebab for their supper on her husband's return. All the while, his eyes were on Elena. She wore a simple white dress that she had made for herself. Its classical line suited her flawless, rather enigmatic face: he carved her eyes in an expressionless, unpupilled gaze; the nose straight; the mouth firm and unsmiling. Her breasts, when at last she took her arms out of her sleeves, were equally perfect and unflawed. The sculptor laboured towards perfection, so that her husband would be as delighted with the bust as he was with the shish kebab – he thought her husband remarkably good looking.

Now and again distant gunfire could be heard. Soldiers occupied many rooms of the tenement; those next door kept them awake with their bawdy songs and shouts, not to mention lovemaking with their whores. There were soldiers, too, immediately overhead. Cracks appeared in the ceiling, from all the rumbles and bangs. Elena was sick of violence.

One afternoon there was a knock on the door and she came dripping from the bath, a towel around her, to answer it. She was expecting the sculptor. But it was the janitor. His grizzled old face was fiery and his breath stank of drink. He made an excuse to come in and then tried to seize her. Her soapy body slipped from his hands and she ran into the bath cubicle. He came after her, clutching at her and swearing. She tried to scream but no voice came, and it would have been useless anyway with the soldiers making such a din next door. She struggled in the blind corner and fell back into the water. He tumbled after her. She was terrified she would drown under his weight – it was one of those huge old-fashioned baths you could easily drown in. She felt him tearing his trousers open. He prised her thighs apart and she felt the thrust. She closed her eyes and did not resist, putting her whole effort into keeping her head above water. She held on to his neck.

He was no better than a beast – and as strong as one – and she had to give way. As they turned to a safer and more comfortable position sideways-on, she tried to send her mind out of her body, through the small glazed window into the blue sunlight. Always she had loved swimming, and below her mind's disgust she could not help a warm weak pleasure in the floating.

She was glad the sculptor did not come that afternoon. She decided not to tell her husband. The janitor was master of their fate. He passed her on the stairs the next morning, and turned away his eyes, ashamed. She told her husband she was afraid of the soldiers, and he promised to get a chain put on the door.

The trouble was with the times. Everywhere there was immorality and unrest, and it entered Elena too. Her husband had to go away for long periods. She asked no questions. When he was at home, she began to feel sympathy for his first wife. It was true, he expected everything to be done for him. She looked at the carving on the mantelpiece, and looked in her mirror. She was born for something different; what it was, she could not say. Maybe it was the good-looking officer from next door who started flattering her and asking her round for tea when his comrades were on duty. He was gentler than the others; at least, he was very polite and charming to her. He made no secret of his intentions, though, confessing that he and his friends had drawn lots as to which of them should try her virtue first. His effrontery at almost any other time of her life would have put her off; but now it excited her. On her third visit to his room she agreed to go to his bed. While they slept, there was a banging at their door, the hook holding it burst from the jamb, and she saw the maddened face of her husband. He walked towards the bed, drawing from his coat a meat knife. The officer grabbed at his holster on the chair by his bed, and fired a shot. Her husband staggered back, surprised by the red bloom at his lapel – his hand flew to his heart.

Again the clang of sirens; Elena's dying husband carried out (and by the very same dumbfounded stretcher bearers, as it happens); the officer taken, quietly, into custody. He wasn't sorry, in actual fact. He was weary of the war, and would get a light sentence, pleading self-defence. The man would not die, he was sure of that. Elena sat in the dark ambulance, holding her husband's terribly cold hand, while the kind ambulance men kept reassuring her it was only a flesh wound.

Chapter Three

One of the carvings on the mantelpiece was a tiny terracotta nude, with squat legs, huge belly, breasts and buttocks. The sculptor had thrown it off as a joke one morning when she had felt queasy. Elena would pick it up and run her finger wonderingly over the round belly, and hope her officer or the old man had not made her pregnant.

She lived on nothing. The weather was warm, and she would go out in the afternoon to sit under the cypresses in the park and watch the marble statues, shattered in the fighting, being clumsily patched together. The replacement limbs didn't quite seem to fit, ever; the natural gestures froze, though often it was hard to tell why.

One day she was caught in a thunderstorm and had to run home. In the hallway she stopped to catch her breath and push her soaked hair back from her eyes. She saw a young man with an 'interesting' face standing there as though waiting for someone. Seeing Elena, he stepped forward, his face white — stepped back. Blushing slightly, she hurried to the stairs.

For a long time she hardly spoke to a soul. Her friend the sculptor had found a new boy to love, and was engrossed. Silence held her, she felt peaceful. Her room was hot. She lay down naked at night, with no sheet over her, the window open. After midnight she would watch the Pleiades drifting towards the earth, and she grew very conscious of her loneliness. When she slept she had a dream that recurred many times. She was running wild, happy, on an island of shady trees under a cloudless sky. The sea was the heart of blue, it almost hurt to look at. She was living with other girls, they reminded her of schoolgirls in her class, in happier days; together they giggled and told tales, and ran and played games. They kissed and embraced, passionately and innocently, they had no need of young men. She wrote verses about her friends, which was strange, as Elena had never written poetry in her life and didn't really understand it. But the verses she made were impregnated with the sea, sky, island and trees, and the limbs and breasts of the girls, distilled them like perfumes, fresh and vibrant. And in her dream she felt her own body to be perpetually scented and fresh, healthy and young: she would never grow old.

Every time, the dream turned into a death wish. She was in love with somebody, sometimes a young man, sometimes a young woman, and her love was not returned. She grieved and wanted to die. She went up to the highest rock of the island – she came to know every olive branch by heart, every turning of the path – and stood on the edge above the dazzling sea, a warm wind blowing her skirt. When she jumped off, all her grief went, she laughed out loud, it was so beautiful to be floating down, the wind catching her skirt and blowing it up round her waist, like a parachute, bringing her down gently to the ocean and the death.

She passed the young man, again, on the stairs. This time he spoke to her, asked if they might talk together. He had found out her room and was on the way up to knock on her door. He had the same pale, intense look, and as she led the way back up the stairs she felt his eyes boring into her back.

When they reached her door, he mumbled something, vanished downstairs again, and returned carrying a bottle of Chianti and two glasses. He poured the wine into the glasses, handed her one, and they sat on the edge of the sofa. She waited for him to speak.

After draining his glass and pouring himself another, he apologized for his intrusion, and especially for his rudeness in staring at her. Seeing her enter the hallway had startled him, overcome him, because she was the image of a friend of his who had died. For a moment he thought his friend had come alive again.

He was a poet, and his young friend had been a poet too. Really they had hardly known each other, thrown together by a sense of being separated from the brutal age. His fingers tightening round the glass stem, the young man described how they had met, how they spent brief hours on the island in the lagoon (the house was surrounded by canals, and in the distance one could just see the wider waters of the lagoon), reading verses to each other, talking, lying in the heat, their faces almost touching. But they had never kissed. He had loved her very much.

One day they had planned to meet, as usual, before the broken caryatids of the senate house, but she had not turned up. Elena knew better than to inquire what had happened. Such experiences were common. She did ask him if he had ever seen or heard of her since – and then remembered his words and said, apologetically, 'Ah, yes, you said she had died.' She put her hands together in a brief gesture of prayer, as if to say she was sorry to have been so stupid.

Yes, said the young man in a low voice, she had died. Long after the terrible event of their non-meeting, he had had word of her living in another city, and a few of her poems appeared in a magazine during a slight thaw in the censorship. As far as he knew, those poems were all that remained. 'But she wrote so many more!' he cried. He gathered his thoughts and told her about her death. News had come to him through roundabout channels. She had jumped from a tenth-storey window to the street. No one knew why. No one even knew which house she had been living in, or under what circumstances. But his beautiful talented friend was dead.

Elena remembered her dream. She was shaken by the coincidence, and told him of it. Perhaps the presence of the young man in the house, her meeting him, his obsessive stare at her because of the extraordinary likeness, had created the dream. In any event, it was very mysterious.

Perhaps it was a consequence of the times that such mysteries were thrown up. Terror and violence and anarchy must create a disturbance in the atmosphere; people became alive with terrific voltage, their force fields were immense; they didn't need to make love; just to look at a stranger, as Elena looked at the young poet, as he looked at her, was shock wave enough, coition enough.

'But why are you so like her?' he said. 'That I don't understand. Are you sure you're not she? Has she come alive again in you?' He seized her hand, and his trembled so much she had to place her other hand over it; and the tighter she held it the more uncontrollably his hand trembled.

Chapter Four

She was to hold his body for the same reason and with the same effect. Not that the poet was weak – effete and languishing as poets are often thought to be; far from it. He was strong and earthy and lively. But he lusted to possess Elena and she would not let him. Never completely. Oh, they would kiss – how they would kiss! She had never been kissed so often, so well. All sense of time would be lost, spinning in a vortex, from the merest tender brushing of closed lips to wide-open cleavings in which her mouth seemed to her a vulva, a great hole of wanting and taking-in.

The presence of death increased sexual hunger just as it increased psychic powers. It seemed to everyone that they had briefly awoken in the midst of a perpetual sleep, and at any moment the needle oblivion would again be plunged under their skin. Who can blame Elena if she seized the moment? Even the soldiers roaring drunk in the next room were not the same soldiers: the former tenants, except for Elena's fortunate lover, had all been killed in one skirmish or another. Besides, her husband had vanished. The doctors, at the apology for a hospital, said that his heart had stopped during the operation to remove the bullet, and he had been rushed to a better hospital in another city. But they wouldn't divulge his whereabouts, and she wouldn't believe them. One could be killed in a hospital as readily as anywhere else.

Convinced that her husband had been killed (reasons were neither needed nor explained), she was not, this time, being disloyal. Rather, what puzzled Elena was why she did not let the young man sleep with her. She was passionate, and she had taken him to her heart.

It was not that she liked being cruel to him; but perhaps a feeling that *he* liked her to be cruel. The hate poems and the love poems came pouring out, and they were beautiful. Even *she* could see that. They were like the lightning flashes that lit up the city sometimes during the hot nights, when they lay alone in their separate rooms; but they were stored lightning. Even when they both slept, when his notebook was closed, the poems still seemed to flicker without thunder on the city's skyline, or beyond the lagoon. The love he had never been able to express for his friend who had jumped from a high window, he expressed to her, her likeness.

Out of his love he wrote a marriage poem to her. Out of his hate he wrote a poem of Attis, a poem of severed testicles and pouring blood. He preferred holding her hand or kissing her, or simply talking to her, to being in the bed of any other woman. She was wise enough to sense that he didn't really want to possess her.

But she wouldn't have been a woman if she didn't get *some* pleasure out of teasing him. She would talk, repentantly, of the officer who had had her. She mentioned the rape and how she had unwillingly begun to enjoy it, in spite of herself. But when he pulled her back on to the bed she stiffened into ice, and warned him that if he forced her she would never speak to him again. And her eyes blazed so, he knew she meant it.

Most tormenting of all, perhaps, was the way she played with the wounded sparrow that plopped through her window one day. Almost certainly someone had caught it and tortured it, breaking its wing. When man was merciless to man, what chance had the poor helpless creatures? Starving dogs and cats wandered the streets. Boys caught them and set fire to them after covering them with petrol. Elena had seen with her own eyes a man take hold of a stray dog and hurl it into a building that had caught fire. And people laughed. She could still hear the dog's scream, and the laughter of the onlookers. But Elena loved animals, and especially birds. She made a splint for the poor sparrow's wing, fed it and nursed it. It got better, though it could not fly far. It hopped around the room, and liked Elena to take it in her hands and rub its back.

She let it go anywhere on her person. It loved to nestle between her breasts, or to couch in the warmth between her thighs. She chuckled when it tickled her, and it seemed to the young poet that she took more pleasure from the bird than from him. He knew it was absurd to be jealous of a sparrow. But then, he was jealous of the air she breathed, the mirror her breath clouded, the clothes touching her skin. He liked – he was forced to admit it – being in this constant state of tumescence and raw anger and jealousy. There *was* something feminine about him; and in Elena, something masculine. Though her hips were large, her breasts were rather small; from the waist up she was quite boyish.

The poet would stagger up to her room, tipsy of an evening, and describe how he had taken a fresh girl off the streets and made love ... or even a fresh boy – as if to say, look how frustration's perverting me! And Elena would nod sympathetically and say she didn't blame him one bit – which made him furious. Once, she touched his prick with her cool fingers, taking pity on him, and his spunk jetted instantly, halfway across the room. And another time she seemed on the verge of letting him in; but he was so excited and overcome that as he touched the entrance he orgasmed. And the little sparrow hopped on to her shoulder and cocked his head at him in a leering wink.

As he lay, biting back his vexation, there was a knock on the door. They hastily adjusted their clothes and Elena went to answer it. It was one of the poet's friends, looking troubled. He apologized for breaking into their evening, but there was somebody downstairs who wanted to speak to the poet urgently. In the entrance hall the poet confronted a long-lost friend from his home town. He was about to embrace him joyfully, but something in the man's face stopped him. The man said that he brought news of his brother's arrest. The poet reeled. More than anyone, except the poetess and Elena, he loved his brother. When he had recovered a little from the shock, he said he would take leave of his girlfriend, gather some things together quickly, and set off for home.

He found Elena crying. The little sparrow had fallen to the floor, dead. She was holding his terribly light body in her hands.

When the poet returned, tired, hunched, and ten years older from his brother's death, he started accusing the girl – on no grounds whatever – of sleeping with the soldiers next door while he had been away. He called her dreadful names – 'whore' and 'slut' and 'filth'. There was no way she could convince him she was innocent.

Chapter Five

Almost as though he wanted her to be a whore, she reflected.

Man called the wolf brother, and his brother, wolf. A few people were doing well out of the chaos, but most were starving. It was winter, the river and canals were frozen solid. The poorly repaired statues in the park were in their wooden overcoats to avoid cracks. There was a renewed clamp-down on the arts, and the poets and painters were forced to find hideaways. The rooms they had lived in filled up with functionaries.

Elena's husband returned – from the dead, as it were. He was long-haired and long-bearded, in dreadful condition. He wouldn't say what had happened to him, but whatever it was, it had changed him. He threw the carvings and pictures into the broom cupboard, and hung a crucifix up. Elena thought it an ugly object – in dark wood except for one large imitation ruby in the centre. The ruby seemed to follow her all round the room, sometimes as a fish, sometimes as an eye, sometimes as a traffic light. Her husband prayed to it night and morning, and made Elena go on her knees and pray too. Though they were terribly short of food, he insisted on dividing what they had and carrying bread to the bawdy soldiers next door – who in fact had plenty. He said they would be blessed for what they gave away; and it was true that a weird assortment of people started turning up at all hours with bread that they shared out. Elena did her best to make them welcome, but it was hard on her. They smelt, they had lice. They saw her husband almost as a saint, listening quietly while he spoke of putting an end, once and for all, to the violence and the corruption.

He didn't want to sleep with Elena. When he did, there was a kind of death rattle in his throat as he came, and he lay like a dead man, and afterwards prostrated himself before the crucifix, begging forgiveness. Elena didn't know what to make of it. She wondered what was happening to her friend the poet. If only she could talk to him!

All the same, she was forced to recognize that her husband had a sense of purpose, now, and was the stronger for it. He exuded power. Sometimes she saw him in a kind of blue aura. And he was doing good in making other men and women feel pure and clean under their lice. She envied them their sense of purpose and meaning. All she could do was help her husband by taking care of his bodily wants. He would come home exhausted, she would pull off his boots that were heavy with snow, remove his filthy socks, and wash his feet. He seemed to like that. When he would not allow her any other liberties – in fact he had taken advantage of another room being vacated to ask the janitor if he could move into it – he would still close his eyes and let Elena wash his feet and rub them very carefully dry.

She felt drawn to confess all her sins. Perhaps she hoped it would stir him to fleshy desire. She told him at last about the old man raping her, and he said he was glad she had submitted to destiny and not fought too hard. Besides, the old man had a lot of good in him. He urged her to let him speak to him about her, invite him down to her room some day so that she could let him love her without rancour, peacefully, show him there was peace and love between them. Elena thought this was very strange indeed, and she hated the idea. But her husband kept gnawing at it. So one afternoon the old janitor came down with a bottle and they had a drink and she let him make love to her, closing her eyes and letting it happen. This time, although it was peaceful, she took no pleasure from it, except that in some peculiar way she was pleasing her husband.

Even queerer – far from welcoming her repentance over sleeping with the officer, he said he was glad she had done so, as it had been the means to self-knowledge and grace. He had visited the officer in prison and thanked him for causing him to die – for his heart *had* stopped – and therefore to be re-born.

Besides, he said, there was more rejoicing over the one sinner who repented than over the ninety-and-nine who had never strayed from the right path. And while she washed and dried his feet, he asked her if she would help the cause by taking men off the streets and then directing them to his room where he would be waiting.

At first Elena refused. It upset her very much. Then her husband started pacing up and down the room and saying there was another reason why he begged her to do this thing. Jealousy had made him commit a terrible sin – threaten a man with a knife. In his heart he had committed murder. He would never feel cleansed of his sin unless he endured the purgatory of giving Elena to all and sundry. He fell on his knees and wept before the crucifix.

She thought her husband was probably unbalanced. But she would do as he wished. To be truthful, prostitution had crossed her mind before – not for any of these garbled mystical reasons but because there was no money. Her husband brought her nothing, there was no work she could do, since women were forbidden by law to take a job. There was no modelling now, nothing. She was growing thinner, beginning to lose her looks. She was tired of subsisting on charity. The way her husband put it made it seem not so bad.

He turned nasty when she said, 'Yes, all right,' striking her a hard blow on the cheek. Then he was all penitence, and carefully bathed her bruise. She became even more certain that his sufferings had 'touched' him. She couldn't follow at all his rambling talk about the world being a maggoty apple, and therefore there was virtue in being the maggot – herself, she gathered – who made the rottenness grossly apparent.

She talked to one of the whores who visited the officers in the next room, and asked her what clothes she would need, where was the best place to attract customers, how much should she charge, and so on. With a little money that her husband managed to borrow from a wealthy adherent, she went on a shopping spree, and came back with a case of clothes and other appropriate items. Even in these times, there were places to get anything you wanted, provided you had the cash and a friend to tip you the wink. If she had to do this, Elena was determined to do it well.

So one night, feeling very self-conscious in her gaudy clothes, breathless with fear and excitement, Elena set off with the friendly prostitute and stood a few yards from her on one of the city's quiet sidestreets. She found, soon enough, that she would not lack for custom. Men of all kinds followed her up the quiet stairs. When they had finished she would ask them, as a favour, to pay a visit to the sick man in the room down the corridor. Most of them did. They liked to think that a whore could be good natured. This way, her husband gained several followers and sympathizers. At the end of each night's trade, he came to her room, made her confess everything that had taken place and kneel beside him in front of the cross, to pray for forgiveness. He was calm and lucid, and she began to feel he was not mad after all.

He said he had to go away for a long time, and not to ask questions. Many of his lice-ridden friends thought he had betrayed them, but Elena stuck up for her husband, saying that it must be important, and he would return.

Chapter Six

Elena walked to the bonfire at the street corner to warm herself. Snow was falling in huge flakes, to join the densely packed snow and ice underfoot. Despite her fur hat, gloves, coat and boots, she became frozen on her beat, even in a few minutes' waiting for a customer. Soldiers were shovelling bones from a cart on to the fire. They were, it was said, not always animal bones. Elena recognized the officer directing the operation. She was glad he had been released, and pressed through the bodies to get near him. His face, turning to her as her hand gripped his arm, looked sterner – or was it only the glow of the bonfire? No, it *was* sterner, more spiritual even, and he had aged. People aged very rapidly in these times.

He saluted her respectfully and then put his hands on her shoulders, fleetingly, glancing towards his men, who had not noticed. 'Have you heard from your husband?' he asked, almost in a whisper. 'Yes,' she lied. A faint smile crossed his face, and he nodded. 'Your husband is a great man,' he said. Elena declined her head. It surprised and pleased her that he was a great man, and two red spots burned on her cheeks. 'I've told everyone he will come back,' said the officer. 'Don't worry, Elena.' Elena nodded. 'I've seen you on the street,' he said. 'It's good. You must go on with it. There are others carrying on your husband's work.' She knew this was true; she was still under instructions to send her clients to visit the sick old man.

He told her to get rid of all her customers by eleven, and he would come to her. By ten-thirty she had pushed her last visitor, still buttoning his shirt, out of her room, and she was washing herself very carefully. She prided herself on her cleanliness; every man was washed away till not a germ remained. She put on a blue dress for the officer. He came, with soldierly precision, as the cathedral bell rang the hour, straddled a chair, and asked her to undress. When Elena was naked he took off his own clothes and lay beside her.

'I'm very tired,' he said. 'Play with me.' She kissed him as the poet had taught her; touched his skin everywhere with her tongue, lips, nails and eyelashes. After fifteen minutes or so his prick was so beautifully distended and bathed with dew that she forgot her prostitute's ennui and wanted him. At that point he took her hand gently in his and held it by his side. 'Now we must rest,' he said. They rested.

Elena could hear the rowdy officers next door, knocking over chairs, breaking glasses, telling filthy jokes, to judge by their roars of laughter. In the candlelight she saw his prick little by little decline. 'That's good,' said the officer. 'Now we can talk.' They talked about her husband, his visit to the officer in prison which had changed the officer's life. He stretched across to his uniform jacket and took a red handkerchief from the pocket. 'Do you recognize it? It's the handkerchief I used to try and stanch his wound. I carry it with me everywhere.'

When he had put on his uniform he stood looking down at her. 'I stood the test,' he said. 'It's good.' Despite her protests he took out a banknote and laid it on the table.

She asked him if she'd see him again and he said, maybe yes, maybe no. Their lives weren't their own. Tomorrow, next week, they could both be dead. He had written, he said, putting on his greatcoat, a short account of her husband's life. They were trying to spread it around secretly. If he left a carbon copy would she write it out six times and hand them on to her customers? Elena said yes, she would, and he took some papers from his inside pocket and placed them beside the money. Then he was gone.

Elena could only endure her clients by trying to love them – in the spirit – however briefly. It was very difficult. They made it so. It shocked her at first to find out how odd people were – men, anyway – how few of them wanted normal sex. When love failed, a sense of humour helped. Sometimes she wished *she* could write. She would have a few tales to tell! The city was full of lunatics, fanatics, charlatans.

Many of her clients insisted on being hurt. The whip that her prostitute friend had said was an essential in the trade was never idle for long. She became so adept at cracking the whip, making crisscrosses of blood leap to their skin, that she jokingly said she could get a job as a liontamer in a circus. Some insisted on being whipped while they were lashed with ropes to the bedposts. Stretched apart thus, one client ordered her to stand above his head, her feet on the pillow, and crack the whip down on his genitals. She was frightened that his screams would attract attention, but there were too many screams everywhere for anyone to take any notice. His genitals a bloody mess, she stopped and asked him if he had had enough, but he told her to go on. This particular man she had to whip into unconsciousness.

Others needed to do things to *her*. Bearing the whip or the cane she thanked the Lord for the extra padding of flesh that women had been given. Sometimes she thought they would kill her, but she clenched her teeth and remembered that she must be obedient whatever happened.

One customer, a mild-mannered dentist, brought along a huge Negro whom he had picked up in the docks, and paid her well to join in a mixed-racial and mixed-sexual orgy. Elena noted curiously that in this case the myth of negroid size was vindicated. While the dentist poked her, the Negro poked him. What sort of men were locked up in the lunatic asylum, she wondered.

Another client, a verminous fellow, was so full of obsessions and prohibitions that though in a sense he was a regular customer he hardly ever actually made love to her. There was nearly always some reason why he could not. Maybe Elena would be wearing blue underwear (or perhaps red underwear). On another occasion he found, when she had taken off her coat, that she was wearing a brooch that reminded him of his mother. Again, if either of them happened to sneeze or blow his nose, this might be a signal for him to hurry into his coat and leave. Or he would count the number of steps he took from the house entrance to her door, and if it was an odd number he would give her a few coins and hurry away. He was full of nervous tics, too, lifting his hand to his glasses a dozen times a minute. And this happened even on the rare occasions when he had walked successfully through his private maze, for he insisted on keeping his glasses on in bed.

One morning when she was resting from her labours, she had a visit from a young painter – he could not have been more than seventeen – who had drawn her a couple of times during the artists' stay in the house. She liked him, he was jolly, fresh-faced and clean, and she welcomed him warmly. He was nervous; it was a risk to walk through the streets, and especially to come here where he might be recognized. But he was tired of being cooped up in hiding. He was afraid, too, that he had lost his gift. Paints were unobtainable, they simply weren't being made any more. Elena asked him if he would like to try, and his eyes lit up. She found a scrap of canvas that had been stopping up a hole in the skirting, and then she got busy with her make-up box. She mixed some of her eye shadow with water, to make blue. Face powder, mixed with a little milk, made a passable yellow. Lipstick, crumbled into water and stirred, made a flaky red. She gave him the brush with which she applied eye shadow, and he started to work. Even making allowance for the miserable colours, it did not turn out very well; his hand was out of practice, and he was still, after all, only a beginner in the art. Elena didn't know what to say. 'Am I that thin?' she laughed, stroking her cheekbones. She saw him bite his lip; he was terribly sensitive. She pretended to like the picture a lot, and propped it on the mantelpiece. 'You've caught the neckline of my dress beautifully,' she said.

Chapter Seven

The customer with the nervous tics had made it into her and reached his paroxysm. When he withdrew, his penis was bloodstained. He stared at it open-mouthed, rapidly adjusting his glasses. 'Oh I'm sorry!' said Elena, sitting up and looking at it. 'I'm sorry. My period's started. It's early.' She leapt from the bed and went to find a towel in the drawer. 'I wouldn't have had this happen for the world.' She fastened her towel on, and gave him a tissue to wipe himself. 'Would you like a wash?' she asked. So few men ever did wash.

'No. No.' He was still gaping at his penis. 'It's beautiful.' Elena had a client who liked to put pepper on his penis, but this was something new. She asked him what was beautiful about the curse. He said it was the blood of life, the spirit's vineyard, and had, besides, magical qualities. He made her take her towel off and he fucked her again, and this time his prick was blood red, crimson red all over. He laughed joyously and said he felt years younger. He gave her twice the money she asked. And there'd be more, he said, if she promised not to change her towel till he saw her again, which would be the very next evening. Elena spent twenty-four uncomfortable hours in bed, grateful (to be honest) for the rest, and taking the chance to copy out the officer's manuscript three times. She had unusually rich dreams. All night she was with the nuns on the mountain near her home. She was very happy because she was allowed to spend all day wandering around the mountain in black; or she was sitting peacefully in her cell, looking out through the bars, that were like slats of a packing case, at a charred maple tree.

The man, when he came back, was in an ugly mood. He had been ill, he had vomited (his face looked green). She had poisoned him with her filthy blood. She was a filthy whore, a witch. She was just a lump of shit. He tore the towel from her, and rubbed it in her face, almost choking her. Then he pulled her off the bed to the floor and put his boot into her stomach. Elena's screams were just another unimportant curiosity in the house: probably a client enjoying her.

Blood spread over the rug. When she recovered consciousness she was in so much pain she couldn't move. Her stomach had swelled out and was black with bruises. She thought maybe her hip was broken. She managed, at last, to reach up for the glass of stale water on the bedside table, and sipped from it. After resting again, she pulled herself by a great effort on to the bed. She fell asleep. When she woke, she tried calling to attract attention, but her calls came out as whispers. She felt so unutterably weak she could hardly move a muscle. She was sure she was going to die. She wondered how much blood she had lost.

It felt as if she was bleeding internally. She vomited, and drifted back into unconsciousness. She lost track of time. Waking and sleeping blurred into delirium. Her body burned, yet froze. She went seeking revenge, flew out of the window, out over the rooftops and domes of the city, into people's houses. Wherever a man snored in sleep, alone or with his wife, mistress or whore, she descended on him and forced love upon him. And at the moment the droning man's prick pumped its seed into her, she bit his neck and drew off his blood. From roof to roof flew Elena, a little stronger each time.

She was married to an undertaker who kept her locked up. But she gazed out of her attic window, and one day a young house painter glanced up and caught sight of her. She signalled to him, and he indicated with a crossing of arms over his breast that he loved her and would rescue her. He put his ladder against the house, climbed up nimbly, shattered the window and burst into her room. She was betrothed to the undertaker but in love with the house painter. It was necessary to persuade the undertaker that she was still a virgin. So she sent her servant (it was the friendly whore) into her husband's bed at midnight when he couldn't tell the difference, he was so drunk. Before dawn she quietly slipped into her husband's bed as her servant quietly slipped out. When her husband awoke and uncouthly fucked her he wasn't at all surprised to find her deflowered. The affair went on. She gritted her teeth and solaced the undertaker when she had to, but even in his embrace she dreamt of the young man and longed to be with him. And every possible chance, they stole away into the woods together.

When the girl woke she found she was under clean linen, and the young painter was sitting by the bed. He smiled his relief and kissed her cheek in delight. Her belly was still monstrously swollen and painful. But she didn't feel that she was bleeding any more, and her head felt clearer. The young painter brought her some broth, and made her eat it, spooning it into her mouth. He said it was impossible to get a doctor, conditions outside were even worse. The only people thriving were the undertakers. (Elena smiled.) He would stay with her until she was better, he said. He did everything for her, even to bringing and emptying the bedpan which he had borrowed or stolen from somewhere or other.

At last Elena felt well enough to walk a few paces to the sofa. While she rested there, the painter asked her, shyly, if she would mind him using some more of her special paints? He would like to paint her just as she was, sick and swollen and wasted. Brushing her hair, while he eagerly set to work mixing the make-up, she promised him that one day they would take a walk up to the hills and she would show him some flowers and herbs you could use to make paints. She teased him for being the complete townee – she had lived between sea and mountain, and had learned lots of things that weren't in books. She slipped out of her bathrobe and he started to paint.

It wasn't a particularly skilful nor a particularly flattering picture, it was – more or less – true to life; a bit like a concentration camp victim, with a high pale forehead (some of her hair had fallen out) and a swollen belly under the small, listlessly hanging breasts. Something like a pear. Something like a foetus, with that seemingly over-large head and gaunt, sad eyes. Elena took one look at it, and asked him to cook some spaghetti.

Chapter Eight

The painter visited her every day, collecting her rations from the market and also, usually, buying her a little treat, if only an apple or an orange. Sometimes he would bring his friends along, young, talkative, good-natured musicians, who made much of Elena, serenading her with guitars. They would beg for kisses, but not really mean it, and were not at all put out when she laughed and pulled her face away, a spot of colour coming back into her cheeks. They did her good. Outside the window it still snowed, but they brought a spring in winter.

Elena thought she recognized the words to one of the songs they sang. Surely the words had been written by *him*? (She remembered the sparrow, and felt sad.) Yes, they agreed, a friend of theirs had written it, a friend who was now in prison. And they fell silent, thinking of him. The poet, they said (for Elena wanted to know everything), had mixed himself in politics. Now he languished in the city's worst prison, the one nobody mentioned without crossing himself and shivering.

When they had drained the cheap bottles of Bordeaux and politely taken their leave, Elena took pen and ink and paper and, though she was very bad at writing letters, composed a careful letter to the governor of the jail begging him to let her visit the poet. This was still the time when officials did occasionally read such begging letters, and therefore there was the chance that once in a blue moon a phrase might strike a chivalric echo. It was worth a try. She sealed the letter and took her first steps out of doors, since her illness, to post it.

A week passed, and then – much to her surprise – she received a reply requesting her to call at the prison on such and such a day at such and such a time. There was no signature, only an official stamp. The painter urged her not to go; the streets were not safe, it was bitter weather, and she was still weak. When she insisted, he begged her to let him go with her. But she knew it wasn't safe for him to be seen; he was taking a risk, he and his friends, even in slinking through the side streets and lanes to visit the house. She put on her faded fur coat, boots and hat, and set off.

The way to the prison lay through the medieval part of the city, by the river. The river was frozen, but no children skated on it. Scenes of horror from the late war were everywhere. Limbs, long unburied, stuck out of deep snow. Long-dead hands implored mercy. Decapitated heads, stuck on pikes, adorned one of the bridges. Passers-by shouted obscenities at her. Elena kept her face hunched in her turned-up collar, and hurried on. She almost fainted with the cold, realized how weak she was still. The sky was leaden, tinged with purple; more snow to come. By three in the afternoon it was dusk. The black hulk of the prison, such a tongue-in-cheek building, came in sight.

The queue by the prison wall seemed to go on for ever. Old women and young children, ragged, listless, turning haunted eyes upon her. No sound came from them, except an occasional dry cough. Elena felt guilty, and hurried past them with her head bowed. At the main door of the prison the guard seemed to recognize her, winked, and let her go through. Perhaps he had been one of her customers. The warder who met her inside glanced casually at the letter she showed him, and in a surly voice told her to follow. They went through long corridors.

She would never forget how blank and pure white those corridors were. The floors, the walls, the ceilings, were all white. But once, she came upon two warders with a mop and bucket, cleaning the floor. There was blood on the floor and on their mop. Dreadful though it was, it reminded her somehow of Christmas. The corridors were colder than the streets. The warder knocked on a door, opened it and motioned her inside.

The room she found herself in was white too, except for a grey filing cabinet and a man at a white desk who was dressed in black. He was bent over a report and she could not see his face. Without looking at her he gestured with his hand for her to sit down, while he went on writing. She sat and looked at the head of grey hair, bent over. She felt tense and she gripped her hands in her lap. His black uniform frightened her, as did the relentless way in which he wrote.

He looked up. She recognized her officer and gave vent to her astonishment by jerking back slightly in her chair. He smiled, and half-rose from his chair to lean forward and offer her his black-gloved hand, the merest touch. She was all fingers and thumbs, and didn't know what to do. He said how pleasant it had been to get her letter, even on such a sad errand, and that he was not surprised by her surprise. 'The slaves are the masters now.' 'Can I see him?' asked

Elena, finding her voice which, to her annoyance, trembled a little. 'You can do more than that,' said the officer. 'You can take him. We've finished with him.'

He stood. 'Come,' he said, and opened a door at the back of the room. She followed him through, into a smaller room. As she entered it she started back with a cry – a huge grey rat had leapt at her, springing back off the wire mesh that held it trapped, a yard from her face. It crouched on the floor of the cage, its fangs drawn. 'Forgive me,' said the officer, taking her arm, 'I ought to have warned you. I'm terribly sorry. One forgets it's there. I promise you there'll be no more shocks.' They went through into a white corridor and into a lift which took them far below ground level, leading to another white corridor. The officer led the way along it and stopped at a cell door, which he opened with his bunch of keys. The strong white light in the ceiling reflected off the walls, making her blink.

She did not recognize the poet. He was curled up on his bunk, curled up like a foetus, and when he heard the door open he drew himself in tighter, and the way his red eyes looked at them reminded her of the rat's expression. She clenched herself and walked the three steps to his side. 'It's me! Elena!' she said, and crouched down to bring her face level with his. He stared at her with terrified red eyes. It was freezing in the cell, and he lay in only his underwear. There were no sheets or blankets. Elena took off her coat and placed it over him. 'I'll send for his clothes,' the officer said.

The terror in the poet's eyes changed, by imperceptible stages, into wonder and reverence.

Chapter Nine

The officer (let us pay respect to his authority and call him the governor) tapped Elena on the arm. She followed him down the corridor to the lift. The lift hummed and took them up again through the prison. On one level, where the doors opened to admit two warders, Elena was unnerved by a scream; and only then did she realize how silent the prison was in comparison with the outside world.

'It will take a while for him to shower and sign a few papers,' said the governor, taking Elena's arm gently and propelling her out into another white corridor. 'In the meantime you can do us a favour in return.' Doors flew apart and all of a sudden they were in a racket of typewriters and printing presses, in an expanse that must have filled almost the whole of one floor of the prison. A hundred secretaries sat typing at a hundred desks, or moved smoothly between them, bearing memos. Displayed around the walls were hundreds of posters. Elena had seen some of them on her walk from the house. She guessed that this room was one of the centres, or perhaps *the* centre, of propaganda, and she felt thrown out of gear by the idea that a prison might contain other activities besides the normal ones of enslavement, torture, interrogation and execution. Almost half the workers buzzing around were women; lately, so many men had been removed from circulation that they were having to abandon the law prohibiting the employment of women.

The governor led her through the desks to a small, quiet room at the end. Motioning her to sit and make herself comfortable, he pressed a button on the desk and spoke into a machine. 'Bring it up,' he commanded. Then he perched on the desk and asked her how she had been, how was business. He was sorry to hear she had been ill.

A girl in a nurse's uniform came in, cradling a baby, and she was followed by a man carrying camera equipment. Briskly he started setting it up. The nurse handed the baby to Elena, who held it gingerly and with wonder. A smile flickered across the governor's face. He explained that they wanted a poster showing a mother with her baby. When her letter had reached him he knew at once that she had exactly the right face, youthful and beautiful and with a quiet determination. Courage even. And her illness brought out these qualities even better. The population had fallen drastically; people were listless about having children in these times. They were going to mount a big campaign extolling parenthood.

'But what if someone . . . recognizes me?' said Elena, blushing slightly.

The governor shook his head and smiled. 'They'd never connect *you* – let's say in bed – with this image.'

She looked down at the baby. It was very pale and silent. It gazed up into her eyes almost without blinking. 'Is it a boy or a girl?' she asked. The governor looked at the nurse, who said it was a boy. The governor added that its mother had unfortunately died in the prison. Elena felt a rush of pity – it was such a dear little thing, but so pale and quiet. She asked what would happen to him. The governor again looked at the nurse, who said he would not live long. He had a hole in his heart.

Of the many poses of Elena cradling her baby that appeared on hoardings all over the city, there is one which slipped through surely by oversight. Elena is looking down at her baby with love, and there is a small but distinct tear on her left cheek.

Chapter Ten

The girl soon forgot her own illness now that she had someone to look after. The poet had her bed and she slept in the armchair or on the sofa. The painter and his friends also helped a lot, bringing food, and cheering him by playing and singing of an evening; but it was Elena who did all the donkey work, nursing him back to strength, feeding him at first with a spoon, like a child.

When he was lying peacefully under a clean sheet, and later when he was able to dress and sit in a chair, his eyes followed her at all times, still with the look of reverence they had taken on when he recognized her in his cell. His gaze made her feel uncomfortable, and she told him so. Then he explained the beautiful realization that had come to him as, fearing another session of torture, he had found himself looking into a strange face, full of compassion and love.

Seeing her so pale and thin, he said, he had recognized her yet not recognized her. That is, he knew she was Elena, but her suffering had given her a more childlike look (and this indeed is true; others had also mentioned it). And it no longer seemed to him that she bore a close resemblance to his poor friend, the young woman who had thrown herself out of a high window. Yet she still reminded him of someone. And instantly he realized that he had seen her – Elena – before, long long ago, when he was a boy and she a girl. At nine years of age, when he had been mostly concerned with train numbers, he had seen a girl of about his own years walking with grown-ups on one of the bridges over the river – had seen her, in a red cloak, and had experienced his first revelation of love. He had not seen her ever again, over the years and the agonies. But Elena's ill appearance in his cell, her tender smile bending to him, had brought that young girl back, and unquestionably Elena was that girl. He asked her whether she had walked over that particular bridge, with her parents, when she was young, and she was compelled to nod her head, recalling her first visit to the city. The poet looked triumphant, as if this confirmed his conviction. As if many girls had not crossed that bridge, as if many girls had not worn red cloaks – for Elena had, too, to admit to a red cloak in her childhood days, when she forced her memory to look back so far.

'And now you have saved my life,' he said simply.

Once he started to get well, he got better quickly. But he would have nightmares that made him start up, crying and panting, from his pillow. She would be instantly awake, and by his bed, soothing him, smoothing his hot forehead, coaxing him to lie back down. He had a recurring nightmare; not of his cell and other more dreadful parts of the prison, as one might have expected, but of a forest, a black pine forest, where wild beasts lurked waiting for him. Elena made him talk about the nightmare, calmly but stubbornly took him through it, every inch of the way, and the nightmares grew less fearsome and finally stopped altogether.

He feared he had lost his gift of writing; but gradually that too returned. One of the guitarists had composed a little song in honour of their hostess. The poet liked it, and asked if he could take some of its phrases and work on them. The guitarist, flattered, readily agreed. The poet made out of it some remarkable verses, likening Elena to a journey into the heart of a rose. The external petals were the lips of her vulva, and the red rose's centre was her mouth – those lips that melded with her eyes to form a delightful, tender, cheeky, kind smile that grew ever more delightful, tender, cheeky, and kind.

Starting life as this sonnet ('Love binds into one volume all its leaves . . .'), the poet's metaphor spilled out of the shapely vessel and started to cut its own bed, seething and dancing, until the unimportant writer was carried along in its torrent. In its fresh form the metaphor fleshed out the leaves of the rose into human characters – became his comedy *The Wedding Party*. His lips moved soundlessly, his hand raced across the page as he 'meditated on death and thereby created new life'. Elena only knew that he was happy and on the road to full health.

Though his use of her vulva as an image in his poem may suggest otherwise, they did not sleep together. This, now, had nothing to do with Elena's wishes. He could not sleep with the nine-year-old girl he had seen on the bridge.

They passed peaceful days. She sewed and knitted; the poet scribbled. In the evenings, usually, the painter and his friends came along with guitars and bottles. They spent a lot of time just sitting, watching the late snow falling outside the window. Elena was well enough to go out to the market, but not yet to resume her own trade; besides, it would have been difficult to do so with the poet living in her room, even though he offered to make himself scarce. Had she done so, it would not have altered the way he looked at her, so worshipfully, for the 'real' Elena was the pure girl, the bride, who filled his pages, 'the good gift on the road to destruction'.

One morning she came back from the market clutching something in triumph. It was a newspaper – two years out of date. The newspapers had long stopped rolling off the presses; and as for books ... But the fruit seller had a son who worked as a labourer who had been tearing down an old house – and lo and behold, stuffed behind a fireplace, an old newspaper! The poet read it with joy, every word, even the adverts. It was a popular paper, with no words of more than two syllables, but still it was a joy to find any print.

When he had finished with it, Elena did the crossword. She had a taste for simple crosswords, but no talent. She got mad with herself for not being able to solve the easy clues, and the poet watched her anger with joy in his eyes. In the end, she had to give up and ask him. But he wouldn't take it seriously. 'Tenants of sewers?' she asked. 'Four letters.'

'Love!' He smiled.

'Shit!'

'No. Love!'

'Leading light – four letters again?'

'Love!'

Chapter Eleven

Snow hissed on the pavements, turned to puddles, to floods. Boughs broke overnight into leaf. As if the spring had caused them, rumours abounded. The queues outside the prisons were said to be growing shorter by the day. Faces long vanished were said to have appeared again, much changed. Thinking they perhaps breathed a little more easily, people hardly dared to breathe at all.

The soldiers decamped from the room next to Elena's, and the poet, unhopefully, went up to the janitor's quarters to see if he might move in. To his amazement the old man was quite civil and said yes. The very next day, he risked going out shopping with Elena, to buy a few things for his room, which the soldiers had left in a terrible condition, and he actually found some tins of paint. More amazing still (and this really told him that something was happening), the fruit seller had a couple of old books on his stall, that his son had come across in his demolition work, and the man in the black uniform had stared at them as he passed but not confiscated them. Though they were much too expensive to buy, the poet had lingered over them reverently. They were children's books with beautiful illustrations.

All over the city there was demolition and building taking place; labourers shouted and power drills droned. Even the old palace was being given a coat of paint. A cheery house painter grinned in at Elena one day, as she sat sewing.

One warm blue afternoon soon after Easter, she walked in the park, where the statues had taken off their winter jackets. The sunshine made even the stiff, repaired limbs look less ungainly. There was quite a throng of poorly dressed but excited people round a new statue, a slim handsome youth, insolently poised with angled hips. Elena joined the admirers, and a man told her it was meant to stand for the rebirth of the city, or at any rate he had heard rumours to that effect. Elena gazed at the statue and something in it reminded her of the bust made by her friend the sculptor. She was almost convinced this must be his work. She sat on one of the seats, closed her eyes, and let the fresh breeze and the warm sun play on her. She felt healthy again, and though she was penniless it seemed to her that life was worth living.

When she got home, a great surprise awaited her. The street was

alive with vehicles, carts, official-looking cars, and even a removal
van. The functionaries in their pin stripe suits were moving out, with
long faces, and the poets and painters were moving back in. There,
standing outside the door, looking as if he owned the place, was the
very sculptor she had been thinking of – black-bearded now, looking
in rude health. He burst into a grin and threw his arms round her
when she came up the steps. And there, behind him, rushing in and
out of rooms with guitars and easels and battered suitcases, were her
other friends from the old days, singing and shouting, banging up
and down the stairs, causing ructions.

They were delighted to see Elena, and she them. A dozen times,
rough arms were wrapped round her and she was lifted into the air!
Bottles appeared and an impromptu party began. They even toasted
the old janitor's health; some said that he had complained about the
soldiers and was not averse to having the artists back. Maybe so: but
also somebody with higher authority must have taken the decision
to move the sober functionaries out. Somebody must have given the
signal that the arts were now to be approved and the artists
treated decently. Anyway a health to the old man! and to the someone else! and to Elena! and to art! The party went on and on. The
sculptor conjured up a vast tureen of minestrone. There was dancing
and the smashing of glasses.

The painter – but let us enjoy his freedom too, and name him:
Peter – was very drunk. So were they all: artists and girlfriends and
even Elena who usually kept fairly sober. Peter was in the poet's room
– let's give him his given name too: Michael. They were swearing at
the piggish manners of the soldiers who had lived there. The furniture
was broken, the walls spattered with wine or blood, the wallpaper
torn. Peter, with a drunken shout, summoned Elena from the next
room, where the dancing still went on, past dawn, and demanded she
take off her clothes. He had taken hold of the paintbrush Michael had
bought, and opened up the pots of paint and was splashing it around
on the walls. He wanted her to model again, he said. Almost before
she could draw breath he had splashed on to the wallpaper the out-
line of her naked body. When she realized he was quite serious, she
protested that it was not very nice having her body displayed per-
manently on the wall, so he compromised by placing her right hand
decorously over her breasts, while, chuckling, he lengthened her
golden hair – it had grown long again, but not *so* long – so that her

left hand could be seen holding a strand of it over her pubic hair. He saw at once, sobering, that it improved the stance, bestowing a spiritual seriousness on the pagan flesh; and he sketched in her features accordingly, refining them. Liberally he splashed the paint around: he had never painted so freely.

Then he told her to put her clothes back on, and this time, on the adjoining wall, he painted her as Venus again, but embowered by trees in springtime. He gave her face Elena's characteristic tilt to her right, but refined her features still further. As though still not satisfied – the poet looked on open-mouthed at such energy and free- dom – he painted her yet again as Flora, covered in flowers and spill- ing flowers from her lap like a sower; and this time with just a hint of sexuality in the slight parting of her lips and the lowering of her eyelids. All around, he sketched in other figures. Peter was still colouring and drawing frantically when the poet was asleep on his bed, and Elena too had crawled exhausted back into her room and fallen asleep amidst a dozen snoring bodies. Not until late afternoon did the spring wood and the ocean look across at each other and express themselves satisfied.

Groups of friends, meanwhile, strolled in the garden behind the house, letting the breeze, the greenness, and the fresh scents clear their heads. The great white dome of the cathedral had never looked more noble. Its bell began tolling for evensong, and had a spritely tone as if it knew this was a very special day in the city's history.

By this time the party had started up again in Elena's room, in a slightly more subdued spirit. Peter sprawled in an armchair, eyes closed, shirt open to the waist, holding a wine bottle. Every now and again he stole off into the next room to gaze at his work, astonished. And then, in a madcap spirit, when Elena indiscreetly told them the story of her rape by the janitor, he carried a paint pot into the bath cubicle and sketched, over the bath, a cartoon of Elena being rav- ished by a swan, with a distinct suggestion of the janitor about the lustful eyes and beak. They all crowded into the cubicle, roaring with laughter. Tears streamed from their eyes, they choked, doubled up. But suddenly all were silent. The old man himself was standing there, beside himself with anger. He had borne one whole night's revelry patiently, but again tonight – it was too much. Then he saw the cartoon, seized a flannel and rubbed it off the wall. His face was a picture, but to their relief he merely stumped off, grumbling. The shock had sobered them up, though, and they spent the rest of the evening sitting around, drinking and talking quietly.

The sculptor asked Elena if he could 'borrow her breasts' – in other words, would she pose for him? He admitted to the statue in the park, and said he had gone over to using male models as it seemed the right image of strength and purpose, for the times. He was at present doing a figure which had to be female, though he was using the young man he was living with for the face, trunk and arms. Elena's breasts, he knew from experience, were perfect examples of their kind, and she'd be doing him a great favour. Elena mumbled a yes, too sleepy to understand really what she was being asked to do.

Chapter Twelve

Summer blossomed with hot days. As the weather held, so did the new freedom. People let out their breaths. It was going to last. Men went to work and came home and ate their suppers, with reasonable confidence they would go off to work again in the morning. They rustled newspapers as they ate breakfast, for newspapers had appeared, without warning, and even one or two bookshops opened. There was the joy of fruitful labour amongst the artists living in Elena's house. They were being paid enough money not to have worries about where their next meal was coming from, and Elena, as their friend and model, benefited indirectly. One result of this was that she ate too heartily and put on weight.

Clearly this is seen in the series of mythological pictures created by Peter during these hot and blessed weeks. Freedom inspired confidence, inspired energy. He scarcely let go of the brush. Down river from the city's heart and just outside its ancient walls was a wood so sheltered and quiet that it might have been a hundred miles from any habitation. One morning, four of them set out for it, carrying a picnic basket – Peter and Elena, and a guitarist friend and his girl. When they had eaten well of their bread and cheese and pickles, and drunk two bottles of red wine, everyone felt sleepy and relaxed in the hot sunshine – all except Peter, who got out his paints, canvas and easel, and persuaded the girls to take their clothes off, and counterpointed them against the still-clothed musician, with the trees as background. Elena, sitting on the grass, looked as succulent as roasted chicken, juicily plump. It depressed her to look at herself, and for two whole days she ate next to nothing. But it was such a pleasure to have decent food and wine, and the sun brought on such a pampered feeling of sensual peace, that she soon forgot her good resolutions. The sensual languor is well caught in later paintings of Elena as Venus: wringing out her hair after bathing; reclining on her bed with a little mongrel dog the artists had taken in off the streets; as Sacred and Profane Love, clothed and unclothed in the same picture, two sisters; as Danaë recumbent, waiting for the shower of gold semen; again, lying in the picnic wood, but this time as Antiope, beside Cupid: a strangely urchin, boyish, subtle and pagan expression on her face that tilts back as if expecting to be kissed. A classical rape scene, in which two men are finding it no light task to carry her, inert and uncomplaining, to bed, finally persuaded Elena that she really must diet.

All this time, she had been living an entirely chaste life. Seeing her portrait gazing out of a thousand posters, a baby in her arms, made her uneasy to do anything to spoil this false image of pure motherhood; though she often felt frustrated, and indeed came to the conclusion that frustration had something to do with her eating so much.

She broke this particular fast on a day of official rejoicing in the city, Liberation Day, selected to coincide with the ancient feast of Ascension. With the latter rather than the former in mind, Elena and her friends decided to join in. They planned a fancy-dress party. All the tenants of the house were invited: the Buddhist monk, the croupier, the supermarket manager, the lady writer of advice columns, the slogan writer, the magician, the whores, the spinsters and widows. It reminded Michael of his *Wedding Party* – everybody in, whether you liked them or not. ('Home is the place where, when you have to go there,/They have to take you in.') Several people asked Elena to run up their fancy-dress gear and she was kept very busy; so busy that she had to stay up all night, on the eve of the party, to make her own dress. She was representing the sea: it was a long blue dress, very tight around the legs, and the skirt was wound around with paper in the form of a mermaidenish tail. She made also a plain blue mask for her face. It was strikingly effective and she felt very pleased with it when she tried it on in front of the mirror.

In the morning, they joined the crowds on the canal bank to watch the water carnival, which was extremely good humoured, boisterous and colourful. Then, avoiding the military parade through the city streets, they hopped into one of the boats following the carnival procession, and enjoyed a leisurely journey along the winding canal, under bridges crammed with sightseers – everybody waving to each other in true holiday spirit. There was much rebuilding and new building going on, they could see a lot of it from the boat, and they were impressed. The sun beat down, the men unbuttoned their shirts to the waist, the women kilted their skirts to their thighs, and they stretched back in their seats and closed their eyes, lulled almost asleep by the splash of oars and the beating sun. Unofficial impromptu events were going on, all over the place. One of the bridges had even been turned into a stage, where an opera was being enacted. It was strange and good, thought Elena, to be gliding into the booming darkness under the bridge and hear a melancholy tenor singing away with might and main over her head.

But after they had glided under another bridge, the poet, sitting across from Elena, stood up, and stared hard at the bridge, looking disturbed, his cheeks drained of colour. He explained later, as they walked back the quite short distance to the house, that he had seen an apparition of his friend, the poet who had jumped to her death. She was wearing black, and was leaning on the parapet, gazing into the waters, looking dreadfully sad. It was undoubtedly her face. He took it as an ill omen that these better times would not last.

They bought some food in a delicatessen near the house, and as dusk fell prepared for the party. It was to be centred in the painters' studio, the largest room, but would send off branches all over the house. Guitars were tuned, presumably by their owners – it was a strict rule of the party that everyone should be masked and would try to disguise his voice, but it is hard to disguise a musician's mastery. Candles were lit, making the room murkier. The masked dancers gathered and the party began.

It was fun not being quite certain who your partner was. Elena thought the man in the gold sun mask was Peter, but she wasn't sure. The burly man in the skull mask might well have been the janitor, because he pressed so lecherously against her and his voice sounded old; but one man's erection, pressed against your dress, is much like any other's. The suave and silky voice behind the cat's mask might well be the poet's friend, one of the enthusiastic young directors of the small Arts Theatre that was about to open; but again she wasn't sure. His hand briefly came into contact with her breast, stimulating her before she pulled away and did up her button. The man who didn't dance but talked to her on some serious, out-of-place topic while sipping a fruit juice might have been the quiet and dignified supermarket manager who had moved into the room above hers: it was certainly none of her artistic friends. She was completely baffled by the slim man in a lion's skin and wearing the snarling face of a lion. She let him persuade her to take him to her room, where they could talk in peace, and let him throw off the lion body (but not the mask) and slide up to her waist the blue fishy-tailed skirt, so tight it was like peeling a glove. It was decidedly a fuck, vigorously animal; though when he did it again it was lazy and like a spell, and it was good that neither knew who the other was. With his hands supporting her plump buttocks, she moved up and down smoothly and luxuriously to his thrusts, like the sea itself. He left her and closed the door softly as she lay in a drowse, marvelling that for so long she had denied herself this pleasure. Ten minutes later she was back in the studio, dancing with a man in the dress of an executioner.

Chapter Thirteen

After heavy rain in August there was a second spring rather than an autumn. The poet spent most of his time in work connected with the new Arts Theatre. Compact and intimate, the theatre was already operating even while the last work of converting it – it had formerly been a church – was taking place. While tradesmen hammered away at the walls, Michael spent the afternoons watching the enthusiastic company rehearsing his play. Often the director would interrupt the action and jump off the stage to crouch by Michael and discuss points of interpretation. Accustomed to working in solitude, Michael enjoyed the feeling of being one of a team, the anxiety of working against a deadline – it made the adrenalin flow – and enjoyed, to be truthful, the flattery of being the centre around which everything turned.

His play, meditated after hours of lying on his bed looking at the refined and spiritual Venus, Peter's mural, was a loose adaptation of the Snow Queen fairy story. He had changed her into a good fairy. Through its virginal and polar whiteness, the Snow Queen's palace was necessary to counterbalance the world's corrupt fertility and to oppose death. The frozen lake in the middle of the state room was the source whereby the grass could spring and be covered with daisies. The Snow Queen rode on horseback through the world, righting wrongs and dispensing justice. Many rich and corrupt people tried to bribe her, but there was no bribe that could tempt her. Her hand was often sought in marriage, but she would temporize, preferring to stay a virgin so that she could give her gentle love to all, even as the snow will cover all the ground. It was very poetic and fantastic, and involved music and ballet too. The lighting expert had a wonderful time creating the effect of the northern lights on the backcloth. The actress who played the central role was excellent in it, as well as good-looking, and the poet started a very pleasant affair with her.

Quite often he would return to the theatre in the evening, either to watch his actress performing in someone else's play, or to enjoy the various other events that went on – chamber concerts, recitals, poetry readings. There was nearly always a good atmosphere, warm, enthusiastic, excited. Afterwards there'd be drinks with his friend the director and other theatricals, and then, home to bed with his actress, as often as not. Even before the great success of his play, he enjoyed an evening of private triumph, when he shared the stage with another young poet. The other poet read in the first half, and was received warmly; but the applause was as nothing compared to that which greeted Michael at the end of his hour-long reading. He had taken the risk of reciting just one work, recently completed. It bore clear affinities to his play, but was much more realistic: an account of a girl living in one room, in difficult and evil times, who makes a meagre living as a seamstress, a model, a prostitute, in a whole series of menial and humiliating professions, yet who somehow never loses her purity, because of the strength of her virginal soul. Though it was set in the past, the important meaning of the work was quite clear to the audience. Every man and woman there felt that the girl was his or her own soul, corrupted by the past, but tonight regenerated. The girl, as the poet described her, was delightfully feminine, and yet boyish too, and he depicted her as often wearing male clothes.

After he had been summoned back many times by a storm of bravos, the poet received the quieter but equally warm congratulations of his friends backstage. He was in a glow of mixed pride and humility, in the knowledge that the work, squeezed out with such despair, was after all, probably, not worthless. He felt sorry for the other poet, and tried to find him to tell him again how much he had liked his poems, but the younger man had slipped away. (And absurdly, he was to drown himself a few nights later.)

The director was throwing a bachelor party. He was a dissolute young man, but finally some girl had trapped him and he was to be married tomorrow. The party, in his delightfully furnished rooms (you had to be very wealthy and influential to boast of *rooms*), turned out as much a celebration of the poet's triumph as a wake for the end of the director's freedom. Everything was of the best. Theatrical gossip flowed, and witty obscenity. The poet carried the glow of a man enjoying intelligent worldly company and good food and drink – though he was not a reckless boozer – between a well-earned artistic triumph and an hour of love with his beautiful and sexy girlfriend. Applause thundered as Michael and the director danced cossack-style round a rose in a glass.

When most of the drink had been drunk and the drawing-room was blue with smoke, the director produced from somewhere a screen and a projector. He invited them to bring their chairs into a semi-circle and look at an interesting film.

It was, of course, a pornographic film. The lighting was poor, and it looked like the work of an amateur. But the watchers, inflamed with drink and sex talk, were not disposed to cavil at the quality. They sat back and enjoyed it, with appropriate rude comments backed with laughter. The film showed a girl being screwed by two men, one of them a big Negro. She sucked the Negro's big cock – there was a good close-up of this which caused much salacious mirth – while the white man fucked her from the rear. Then the action was reversed. The film climaxed with a feat of involved coupling, or trip-ling, a three-backed monster.

It was clear from several of the remarks – one had to expect this at a theatrical gathering – that a few of the guests found the massive lithe Negro more tempting than the girl.

The director was laughingly turning aside the questions – had he bought the film? Where had he bought it? Had he made it himself? – when the poet, unnoticed, slipped out. He walked the streets, smok-ing cigarette after cigarette. What had disturbed him so much – perhaps more than anything he had ever experienced, including im-prisonment – was that he was sure he recognized the girl. It was Elena. He was sure it was her face. And that gesture of pushing her hair back from her eyes with both hands, as if putting aside a veil, it was a characteristic of Elena's. Admittedly the hair was black, or looking black, but this could have been an effect of the bad lighting. And anyway Elena had been known to try out a different colour. He would know those eyes, and those lips, anywhere. They were Elena's. It could not be Elena, and yet it was.

It was all very well knowing she had made love to men, knowing even that she had sold her body. But to see it, with his own eyes, this was unendurable. To share the feeling of those men as they screwed her, and to share her orgasms. To know what she really meant when she said 'we made love'.

He burst in on Elena in the middle of the night, shaking her awake. She was angry at being woken, and passionately denied ever having made such a film. She burst into tears, faced with a possibility so monstrous it was not to be thought of. The poet believed her with-out believing her. He looked into her angry face and wondered why she so moved him. It was not that she was beautiful. She was quite plain, really, and overweight. He longed to climb into bed with her, but remembered – as if he could ever forget it – the film.

Soon after, he started to discharge from his genitals, and was con-vinced that Elena had passed on an infection – which was absurd, as he had never slept with her.

Chapter Fourteen

That winter Elena re-married. Her new husband was the polite and sober supermarket manager she had talked to at the fancy-dress party. There was a very simple ceremony. Peter, and a clean-cut traveller for a frozen foods company, were the only witnesses. Her friends wanted to throw a party, but neither Elena nor her husband wanted any fuss.

No one asked any awkward questions about Elena's first husband. She herself was convinced he was dead, or at any rate would never return to live with her. Probably he had been arrested and sentenced to a long term 'without right of correspondence', which was the equivalent of a death sentence. Most people who had known her husband agreed with her, even if they did not say so openly. His ideas, though, were very much alive. Elena had given the supermarket manager a copy of the 'short life'. He had been deeply impressed.

She was not in love with him, but respected his simple virtues. She could see he was a good man. After the fancy-dress party he had taken her for walks, and had treated her in a very proper way. He did not know she had been a prostitute and Elena saw no reason to trouble him with the knowledge.

When he proposed to her, she considered it a long time before agreeing. She made up her mind to it one night when he took her to the open evening at the university observatory. An odd incident settled the issue. She had looked through the telescope and seen Jupiter and its moons; then she turned to her friend in the dark to make some comment, but she was speaking to a total stranger. She felt awfully embarrassed. Her friend had moved away for a few moments. And saying 'I'm going to have to find a toilet', straight into a stranger's face, told Elena that all her life was like this, that no one was really close to her, and she was lonely. So, on the way back to the house, drifting in the canal bus, she had said she would marry him. In his sober way, he was very pleased. It seemed the right thing to do at his time of life, no longer in the first flush – to marry some decent woman and start a family. He liked the old proverb 'a man is for meat and a woman is for broth'. He could well provide the meat, and

Elena promised to be a good housewife. He took her to the room where his old parents lived, and they approved his choice.

So here was Elena married again and sharing her life with a man. Such changes were commonplace occurrences, and after a while it hardly seemed much different, to Elena. She was not sentimental and had no regret over the past. She cooked, and sewed, and knitted, and cleaned. Two or three times a week they made love. Her husband was not a passionate man, and he was also shy and inexperienced. Elena would not have said they had a wonderful sex life, but it was adequate, and might improve with time. It was not the most important thing, after all.

The only person who was really disturbed was the poet. He refused her invitation to be a witness. They heard him walking about his room but hardly ever saw him. When she bumped into him on the stairs he turned his head to the wall. Partly his moroseness had nothing to do with Elena, at least directly. On its first triumphant night he was the only person convinced that *Snow Queen* was a failure: he had to move it towards ambiguity, complexity, darkness. Very slowly and tortuously it was 'Negro-ing', and although the self-torture was necessary it also irritated him, as if he were a small boy fingering a scab.

But clearly Elena's marriage did not improve his temper. Nobody else seemed to mind, or even notice very much. There were always new partnerships being forged, in these still-uncertain times. There were men in the house who were not quite sure whether they were living with their first, or their second, or their third wife. With so many people living in single rooms in the house, changes of partner could be brought about with a minimum of fuss. People every week were changing rooms. An hour's bumping about on the stairs, and Elena's new husband was firmly ensconced in her room – on the whole it was the nicer – with his familiar and much-loved things added to hers.

This was the main change she noticed. Her room was fuller and more comfortable. It had a solid, respectable, even bourgeois look, with his fine set of old chairs, and above all his piano. For her husband liked playing the piano; nothing flashy, but sensible pieces. He had a rather heavy tone, but played very correctly, and with a certain stately feeling. There was also his painting of tulip fields in spring, with the gilt frame. He had found it in an antique shop and was very fond of it. Seeing how uncomfortable he was with the bust, the ter-racotta nude, and the nude sketch Peter had given her, she stowed them away again in the broom cupboard.

Peter chuckled when he noted these absent friends. 'I'll paint you something he'll like,' he said, 'as a late wedding present.' While her husband was at work, he set to and painted her in a neat sober brown dress, standing by the piano, on which was a bowl of flowers. He took great care over it. It was a good portrait of the girl, but this time Peter had made everything else seem of equal or even greater importance, including the piano, the flowers, the flower bowl, the painting of the tulip field on the wall, the chairs and table in the foreground, a blue vase on the sideboard, the curtained window. He framed the picture, wrapped it in brown paper, and presented it to her husband. When he unwrapped it he blushed with sincere pleasure. He was proud of his wife, and of his piano, and of the room that was their comfortable home till they could afford an apartment. And here it all was, in the painting. He shook Peter's hand and asked Elena, who smiled at his pleasure gratefully, to make their friend a cup of tea.

She made tea also — and little buns — for her new husband's old friends who visited them regularly on Sundays, and irregularly during the week. They came to talk about serious concerns, and often to meditate in silence. Elena knitted, and had her own more trivial and vastly more serious concerns to meditate about. It was a quiet life, not unpleasant. They went for walks by the canal when the weather allowed it, and once he took her to see *Snow Queen* at the theatre, but he was uncomfortable at so many flashy effects and also some of the dialogue, which was inclined to bawdy. Elena could see there would not be many visits to the theatre. But still, she could always fly down to the artists' studio during the day, and have a glass of wine and a laugh. Christmas was a very quiet time, spent with his parents and brothers. But inside her, she felt a tiny life beginning to stir, and she was glad to sit quietly.

At least there would be enough money to have a baby and bring it up decently. There were a few ominous signs, again: one day, distant gunfire was heard. There were strikes and demonstrations. The artists got fewer commissions and were buying beer instead of wine. But if things grew worse, her husband would surely be all right. People would always need food.

Chapter Fifteen

The signs were bad: rumours and counter-rumours, spoken by people who glanced over their shoulders; screams from the street; the occasional tread of boots climbing and descending the stairs in the middle of the night. It was said that there were longer queues outside the prisons. Posters were torn down and defaced – including the ones of Elena depicting motherhood. If this hadn't happened so suddenly and in conjunction with sinister events, she would have felt relieved by this particular defacement, for now that she carried a child of her own the posters seemed a travesty.

The newspaper (there was only one) changed its editor and proceeded to mount a harsh campaign against public immorality. First it attacked the bars and cabarets for their 'licensed corruption'; next it was the turn of the Arts Theatre, 'a scandal to all decent citizens for its propagation of vice'. The letter columns became crammed with the views of decent citizens, supporting the newspaper's brave stand, and demanding that the authorities take action forthwith. In due course the bars, cabarets and theatre were closed, and the letter columns filled with congratulations to the authorities for cleansing the city's putrid air, but pointing out that the root of the depravity had scarcely been touched.

Elena's husband approved of the measures the authorities had taken, but she was frightened and no longer glanced at the paper after her husband had left for work. She shut her ears whenever he, or his friends, referred to the campaign. But one day she bought herself a bag of chips for her lunch, after visiting the market, and when she unwrapped the old newspaper a small news item caught her eye and made her heart beat faster. It simply said that the authorities had launched a drive against prostitution; it was not enough that whores had vanished from the streets (such-and-such a spokesman had said), they must be pursued into the sewers where they were biding their time. Elena looked at the date at the top of the page, and found the newspaper was three days old. She made herself a cup of tea, which calmed her nerves a little. All might be well. But she packed a small bag to be on the safe side.

And the following day there was a knock on her door and a polite policeman asked her if she would accompany him to the police station. They passed the painter as she followed the policeman down the stairs; Peter looked shocked, and Elena gave his arm a quick squeeze of reassurance. At the station they checked her identity against the files of known prostitutes and she found herself being driven in a black Maria, with several other young women, to an unknown destination. There was none of the chatter which one expects when women, even if they are strangers, are thrown together: each face was frozen in its own terror.

But the reality was not so bad. The correction centre imposed a spartan regime of physical training and moral re-education, hard beds and little food. But at least the guards were women and they did not mistreat the inmates. The worst indignity, for Elena, was having her hair cropped short. But it would grow again. After three weeks, she found herself being given her clothes back (she was glad to get out of the ugly uniform) and released. In view of her pregnancy they were not assigning her to useful production work – they told her to be a good wife to her husband and prepare herself to be a decent mother.

But when she turned the key in her door and entered her home, she found it stripped of all but its original furniture. There was an envelope on the bed. Slitting it open she found her husband's wedding ring, and a sizeable banknote. Elena had half-expected this, and knew she deserved it. She really ought to have told him. What she could not understand was that she felt very little sadness – even a tiny relief. It was good to have her own things round her. Straightaway she took off her clothes and had a long, luxurious bath.

When she felt more herself again she went downstairs to the studio. Several of her friends were there, and they greeted her with relieved embraces; but after toasting her freedom, in flat beer, they lapsed into gloom. Every day they were expecting to be locked up too, or driven out of the house and dispersed. Miraculously their weekly cheques were still coming through, just enough to keep body and soul alive. They were drinking the last barrel of beer and painting inoffensive subjects, hoping to weather the storm.

Elena asked about Michael, and they said they had not seen him for ages. He stayed in his room with the door locked. They could hear him pacing the floor, but he wouldn't answer to their knocks. They thought he went out at night.

She herself heard him pacing his room. She knocked on his door and on the wall by her bed, and called to him; but without response. She went out to the market and on her return put some groceries in a cardboard box and left it outside his door. In the morning the box had gone. She hoped no one had stolen it. He continued to refuse to acknowledge anyone, she continued to leave him food and drink. Sometimes, when she was finding it hard to sleep, she thought she heard him go out, and return, in the middle of the night.

She was woken in the small hours by a banging at the door enough to raise the dead. Still half asleep she pulled on her dressing-gown and went to the door. There were two burly men in the familiar black raincoats and hats, and behind them the white face of the old janitor. He vanished, as the two men pushed past her without a word and started ransacking the room. They brought various canvases and bits of sculpture from the broom cupboard and placed them on the table. One of the men told Elena to get dressed. They sat, chewing gum and staring. She packed her bag hurriedly and they bundled her out of the house into a black car. Elena, though numb with shock, and as if drugged, still recognized the prison whose main gates opened to take her in.

Over the next few weeks – though she lost track of time – she became accustomed to the sound of beatings, and of screams more dreadful than she had ever heard before. She grew unclear whether the screams belonged to other women or herself, whether it was her body they were dragging along the corridor, wearing only her shift, or other bodies she caught glimpses of. Nearly all the guards were men, and nearly all the prisoners whom she glimpsed were women; but on one occasion she was dragged to a cell in another part of the prison and confronted with a bald and naked, curled-up embryo whom she dimly recognized as the former governor of the prison. Then, and later through the relentless interrogation beneath the eternal light, she realized that someone had associated her with the governor and spotted the resemblance to the woman on the posters. They demanded that she confess to all sorts of crimes committed under the governor's orders, but she could think of nothing to say, even when they pressed needles into her breasts and under her fingernails.

They hammered away also on the subject of a crucifix that had been hanging in her room. Her mind was so clouded with pain that she simply could not remember what had happened to it; but of course they did not believe her and pressed lighted cigarettes to her breasts. *Why* was it important anyway? They wouldn't tell her.

They flashed obscene photos she couldn't recall having posed for in front of her eyes, and threatened to mutilate her beyond ever doing such lewd acts again, unless she confessed what they wanted. She desperately wanted to confess, but they wouldn't tell her what she was supposed to have done.

After every rare, exhausted sleep she would wake up in the icy cell with one thought alone, a prayer that she might be faced by the kindly interrogator who kept pleading with her to confess her own and the governor's wickedness in order that she be spared further suffering. But more often than not she would be looking up into the demonic eyes of the other man, who drew blood from her, stamped on her naked feet, or punched her breasts. She knew this sadist. This was the man who had been obsessed with her menstruation and had left her to die in her own blood. Facing him, she could only long for unconsciousness, but it was always years coming. Once, she heard a gun go off in the next room, but if this was meant to frighten her it did not succeed, since she would have welcomed death.

The sadist tried putting an electrode in her vagina, and when she recovered consciousness he raped her. She woke up in the night thinking she was dying, but she was only bleeding her baby. A guard, less inhuman than the others, saw her on the floor when he peeped through the judas hole, and had her taken to the prison hospital.

Someone found out the name of her first husband. That name was still held in respect, and Elena found herself released.

Chapter Sixteen

Perhaps Elena's greatest strength was her ability to forget the past and put her best foot forward. She was hardly the same woman, she would carry the scars to her grave, but thanks to the kindness of her friends and her own determination she was soon on the way to health. Among the friends who cared for her and talked at her bed-side for hours was a man in dark glasses whom she did not at first recognize.

But when – after drawing the curtains – he removed the glasses and stared at her with red eyes, she saw it was Michael, and she held up her arms and clung to him. The reason for his weeks of with-drawal was really quite simple, he had been giving his whole heart and soul to a long poem. He had recoiled into himself, aware and ashamed of having been carried away for a time by the false glamour. His revision of the play had turned eventually into a long lyric poem about Persephone's darkness. Through it, he said, he was trying to explain 'this' – and he twitched the curtain back to look out at the city, its towers, domes and tenements, but the evening light made him screw up his eyes. Writing obsessively day and night in his murky room had damaged his sight. He had scarcely stopped to eat or drink, though he was grateful for the unknown friends who had left food outside his door. Sometimes, he said, he had gone out in the dark, when he would meet no one, and eaten a meal in some grimy all-night diner. But even then he had bolted the food down to get back to his underground lady. He had started to see thin spiders running all over his room, but they were in his eyes. Now he had finished the poem, it was the rest and relief he had longed for; yet he was unhappy because there was no longer a meaning to his life. He felt sure he had lost his gift and would never write another line.

Graffiti were chalked over the pronouncements of the new regime; the newspaper stopped appearing and there were street battles for three days. Then the newspaper came out as a single sheet, announcing victory, with large photos of heroic leaders who had been murdered in the counter-revolution. The new editor called for the sternest punishment of the murderers and asked the people to demonstrate their support at tomorrow's victory celebrations. Within minutes, it seemed, the people had poured out on to the streets, with all their pent-up instincts ready to be unleashed. There followed the most disorderly period of licence the city had ever known. The bars were thrown open, their cellars raided, and the liquor stores' windows smashed. Drunken gangs roamed the streets, shouting and singing. The wife of one of the artists, hurrying home, was set upon by three youths and raped in the alleyway. Her story must have been repeated a hundred times in one evening in the city. From Elena's window, as night fell, they could see fires burning in two districts where bonfires or fireworks had got out of hand; and they burned on uncontrolled, as all the firemen were drunk.

The licence became general over the following weeks. Evidently it had the approval of the authorities. Casinos, cabarets and strip joints re-opened, or opened for the first time. Whores came out of hiding – there were several living in Elena's house. Previously respectable wives could be seen, on occasions, climbing the stairs, tipsy, hanging on to the arms of officers or seedy businessmen. One could hardly blame them for deciding to cash in on the quantities of paper money that seemed to be floating down from the sky with the snow – though little enough of it came to the artists who were Elena's friends. Their money had stopped coming through and their initial hopefulness turned again into brooding.

Elena found a job as a waitress at the Arts Theatre. It had been reopened as a kind of artistic cabaret, with tables and a bar in place of rows of seats. The art consisted mainly of striptease and other dubious items. On two nights a week plays were performed, but with little respect for the author (*Snow Queen* was revived as a nude spectacle, and with a cheap happy ending tacked on). Elena soon found that her 'waiting' consisted mainly of sitting with men and persuading them to buy expensive drinks – in reality coloured water. Since the customers were usually buffoons or downright villains (the prisons had disgorged murderers and con-men as well as martyrs), she did not mind the deception. At least it earned her money with which she could keep herself alive and the poet too. Her customers expected her to take them home with her at closing time, and she was taught to encourage this expectation (they spent more). Sometimes, if she felt more than usual contempt for them, she did find herself taking them home. When she got them to bed she was not above leading them on by promising even finer, indescribable pleasures if they paid extra. Once or twice, she despised a slimy bedmate so much that she extracted his wallet before pitching him drunk out of the room. The money was shared with all her hungry friends, and she regarded herself as no more than a Robin Hood. She was working terribly hard. By day, besides her own tasks of washing clothes, cooking, cleaning, and so on, she typed out Michael's long poem, one-fingered, on a second-hand machine she had picked up cheap. He wanted it finished quickly so he could send it off to a sympathetic editor in whom he had good hopes. He grew angry if she couldn't decipher his scribbles and crossings-out, or was tired and had to stop. He wanted her to read to him too, so that she started to see her own thin spiders.

The customers' appetites craved more sensation. To keep her job, Elena had to do really unpleasant things, appearing nude on the stage and assisting in live sex acts. As a climax she was taught to walk between the applauding tables, collecting tips in a black top hat. She grew used to their flabby pinching fingers, skilled at hissing 'fuck off' through an unmoving smile. The customers growing stingier, the management introduced the novelty of having Elena pick up silver coins from the edge of a table, using peculiarly inappropriate muscles. One night, heading for a bright coin being waved by a laughing, oily businessman (his ash-blonde giggly mistress making a half-hearted attempt to pull down his arm), Elena caught sight of a man in dark glasses sitting alone in the corner. A blush flooded her cheeks and she hurried past the disappointed businessman and his secretary to grab her wrap from the bar. Slipping into it and tying the belt tightly she went to sit with the poet. There was a food stain on his shirt, he slumped over an empty bottle, stared into the dark glass. Elena touched his arm and spoke his name. She was glad he could not have seen her performance.

Chapter Seventeen

Order came back to the city. Decent citizens wrote to the newspaper to say that they understood, but deplored, the excesses which had greeted the return of freedom. Cabarets, brothels, casinos and strip clubs were brought under strict control. The burgeoning media proclaimed that the cult of irrationality must never be allowed to return; henceforward reason and orderly economic planning must prevail. Permits began to be required for just about everything. 'Progress must be our catchword' – when Elena read to Michael this headline from a report on the party congress, he burst into tears.

This was not as silly a response as one might imagine. Evening by evening (Elena had found a job as a typist in one of the Ministries so her days were occupied) he listened more intently and more anxiously as she read him the newspaper. Something strange was happening to its style. Elena could not pick it up, but he, with his trained ear, could. But it was only when articles and letters began to appear demanding a rationalization of the language, in the interests of better and more efficient communication, that he fully understood what his ear had sensed. Certain ways of saying things were disappearing. He noticed it on the radio too, and even in the street. Subtler, more richly connotative forms of expression were being replaced by terse denotative statements. He understood, now, why the sympathetic editor had returned the typescript of his long poem, observing that its language was archaic and obscure and advising a revision – that day when he had gone to the Arts Theatre to drown his sorrows and had been taken home by Elena, dead to the world.

Other people were not noticing what he noticed; or if they did, they thought it high time. General approval greeted the report of the Education Secretary's inquiry, which advocated sweeping changes in the teaching of language, including a simplification of the dictionary and the grammar book, balanced by a call for firm discipline and high standards in teaching the simplified programme.

Winter passed into summer. A dead weight hung over the city. People got up, went to work, came home, listened to the radio and read their magazines, went to bed, got up again. Most of them appreciated the well-ordered life, even if the endless form-filling exasperated them.

There was little singing or laughter in Elena's house. Many of the artists, tired of having their work rejected by committees, gave up altogether, took jobs in advertising, films, or communications. Others decided to produce the lifeless exact copies of former masterpieces that the new Ministry buildings were demanding as status symbols. As for Michael, his affable editor (who ran the only poetry imprint in the city) silenced him more effectively than any persecution would have done. The editor would stand him a lunch, then say 'Sorry old chap'. He tried to write in the prescribed manner, but it would not work. He broke his pencil in half and threw away the pieces.

He had started to see his actress friend once more, and he wrote a poem about her cat, and another very simple poem about rain falling on city roofs (it came to him when she was walking him home one night). He had high hopes for these. Surely nobody could object to them either in style or theme. Even a small cheque for a magazine appearance would be encouraging. But the affable editor sent them back, saying they were too emotional, and wishing him well for his birthday. Elena was angry, because she liked these poems – liked them, if truth were known, more than the endless poem she had typed out for him.

Elena's task in the huge open-plan office was to type out the memos dictating this or that change in production policy and pass them on to the underlings who had to ensure the commands were carried out. It was very boring and she brightened her life by trying to make mistakes wherever she could do so without too much risk of detection. And one day she was able to change an order for the fivefold increase in boot production to an order for a fivefold increase in book production. That is why the dreadful shortage of boots continued throughout that year, while the bookshops suddenly became flooded. And why the affable editor, who had just sent to the newspaper a less than affable article criticizing subjective emotionalism in poetry – and mentioning Michael by name as a man of talent who had gone off the rails – made a personal call on the poet and asked him to translate several classics. It was better than nothing, and he agreed. Elena typed out some of his translations during lunch hours, as a change from the eternal memos and directives. She liked the part about the queen who wove a wedding dress all day and unpicked it all at night. In her own way, she was trying to do the same, fouling up the works whenever she could: she had Michael and his girlfriend rolling on the floor, almost, with the telling of her droll 'mistakes'.

It was a quiet time for her, mostly. In a way she was glad, after all the disasters. Sometimes she dreamt of the baby she might have had, but she forgot all about it by morning. She had a boyfriend, a clerk from the office, for a while. They might go to a film, or for a walk in the park, where it upset her, slightly, to see every twig clipped, every leaf swept up. Her lover was a bit like that: every hair in place. The lovemaking was pleasant enough; but when she realized she was studying his curtain material over his shoulder, she stopped seeing him.

She was popular with her workmates. Several of them started coming round of an evening for a cup of tea and a chat. They were earnest young men and women, eager to discuss social problems. The rights of non-Caucasians and of women got a full hearing. They appeared to respect Elena, saw her as the 'centre' of their discussions, which was flattering to her, considering her lack of formal education. She had enjoyed more experiences (most of them bad), and they thought her very wise and sensible. She felt uncomfortable at the way they sat on the floor around her, as if she were a queen bee. Of course, not all of her experiences were of a kind that she wanted to talk about. They were rather a priggish lot, and pompous; and two or three of the young men were too idealistic and romantic for Elena's taste. They would harangue the group about so-and-so's new novel, and gaze adoringly at their hostess as they waited for her opinion. But Elena, who never read novels, would turn the conversation adroitly to something more down to earth, such as the slightly smarter dresses that were beginning to appear as a result of one of her mistakes.

Chapter Eighteen

Not that she had much time to worry about dress. Besides her work, and looking after a half-blind man (Michael had fallen out with his girlfriend, and more and more leaned on Elena), she was now fitting in shopping and household chores for the old janitor, who had suffered a slight stroke. During one of the earliest 'at homes', discussion had been interrupted by a thud somewhere over their heads, and some plaster had fallen. A heavy electric light bowl, it transpired, had worked loose from its fittings and crashed down, just missing the old man's head, striking his shoulder before smashing to fragments on the floor. The shock to his system was worse than the actual injury, and his stroke had occurred soon after. He could walk about his room with the aid of a stick, but found it impossible to climb stairs.

So Elena, with two or three kind-hearted tenants, was helping out.

She had small reason to be kind, and precious little thanks for it either; but she helped because *somebody* had to; and 'better the devil you know than the devil you don't know'.

She worried a lot about the poet. He was plunged in gloom most of the time. The newspapers she read him never failed to depress his spirits further. There was a massive correspondence, spontaneously begun, demanding that art reflect the views of the man in the street and condemning writers who took up an arrogant, anti-social stance. One letter, signed 'Rose grower', mentioned Michael by name; the outraged citizen said he had come across a poem, or what purported to be a poem, comparing a rose with a young woman's 'private parts'; he was appalled that such a work might fall into the hands of the young. The letters, and associated leading articles, shared a common, and peculiar, lexicon of abuse: 'mystique', 'subjective', 'disgraceful', 'disgusting', 'aberration', 'deviant', 'muddle and murkiness', 'intolerable facts', 'storm of indignation', 'criminally irresponsible', 'at odds with reality'. Such critical analysis carried, of course, its own in-built proof. On a radio programme about the arts in society, Michael's affable editor said that some of the more recent work by the talented author of the *Snow Queen* had literally made him 'vomit'.

The poet could not understand why people had become antagonistic to him in particular, since none of his more recent work, apart from the innocuous translations, had ever appeared. Now even the translations had trickled to a halt. Rather ironically, just at this time, a new reference book gave him this terse entry: 'formerly a poet, author of *The Snow Maiden*, but now a translator'. On the evening of the day when a friend had telephoned him with news of the reference item, Elena found him standing in front of the open window. 'Shall we jump?' he said. She took his arm firmly and led him back to his chair. Things could only improve, she said. He said, No, they would get worse. But she was right, it was cowardly to jump. Our lives were not our own. We were not born for happiness, but for some other destiny.

Elena rather doubted such high phrases; she didn't know why she was on this earth; but she kept quiet.

He relied on her to keep him going, worshipped the ground she trod on, and was irascible with her. He abused her in vile language, enraged not only by the imposed silence but also by the difficulty he had in seeing. His eyes were very slow to improve, and he refused to let a doctor look at them. At most he would let Elena apply some drops she had bought at a chemist's — which were probably doing more harm than good. He had always used his keen sight to the full — witness his poem comparing his vision to sharpened scythes — and now the dark glasses stood between him and the world, preventing him from writing even in the priest hole of his mind.

She tried to cheer him up by taking him, one Saturday, on a picnic to her favourite wood. But this visit made them both miserable. The trees had mostly been cut down to make a formal garden round a lake, and gigantic statues had been put up glorifying the founders of the revolution. They felt so sick they threw their sandwiches to the ducks, and came home.

The campaign of vilification moderated slightly, or shifted course. A new and apparently more gentle term gained prominence in the critical lexicon: 'neurotic'. Elena's workmates had not, for some time, visited her of an evening; and at work they had kept their distance. But all of a sudden they were friendly again and asked if they could come round. One of the idealistic young men, pimply and in rimless spectacles, started to talk about his admiration for Michael — didn't he live in the next room? Wasn't he a friend of Elena's? The others, too, expressed their enthusiasm. Could Elena arrange an intimate poetry gathering? — it would be such a change. Next week perhaps? Or why not this very evening? They knew he was in: could hear him moving about, from time to time, in his room.

Elena's scalp prickled, but she thought it prudent to pretend to go and pass on their invitation. She urged him to say he had a headache. But the poet, in a desperate mood, ready for anything, insisted on taking them at their word.

The guests bubbled with enthusiasm as they welcomed the poet. It was such an unexpected delight and honour! Michael stared hard through his black lenses at the bespectacled idealist, as they shook hands. (He told Elena later that he had had a sudden idea for a poem about Judas, and his happiness at the idea led directly to the reckless vitality of his reading.)

He knew his poems by heart. He began by reciting a section from the long Persephone poem. Elena, watching faces, saw that they did not understand it. He then spoke some of his early erotic poems, which they obviously understood only too well, shuffling in their seats and appearing thoroughly embarrassed. The rose/mouth/vulva poem came next. Glances fell into laps. He then read to them the only recent poems in which he took any pride at all: the one about the cat, and a filthy ballad concerning a bishop who opens a relic case containing a turd of the Holy Virgin, and reels back disgusted with the smell. (Elena recalled an occasion when her lavatory was not flushing properly, and how surprised she had been by his reaction to one of her stools floating back up.) As though indifferent to or unaware of the shocked silence, Michael finished with a scurrilous mock-heroic ode to one of the newly erected gigantic statues.

The young idealist broke the painful silence. Blushing scarlet, he summoned up an expression of gratitude, and asked if he might show the poet some of his own humble verses one evening. The poet took off his dark glasses, gazed straight at him with his inflamed eyes, and told him he would be welcome any time.

Elena tried to break the evening up, but ran into hostility from Michael, who was thoroughly enjoying being outrageous — picking his nose, scratching his groin, farting. One of the young ladies asked him why he needed to use such crude expressions in his love poems, and Michael said in reply that 'cunt' was a good, heroic word because it was incorruptible, wholly itself, and she mustn't be ashamed of hers. He got down on all fours and started barking like a dog, crawling round, sniffing, and thrusting his head up the skirt of the young lady who had rebuked him.

The young man brought his hack verses the very next evening. The poet was friendly and noncommittal. The young man took to dropping in at all hours, questioning Michael on his beliefs. Michael answered everything with perfect honesty. Soon the young man was dropping all pretence of being interested in poetry. He lolled around till past midnight, rudely and arrogantly, waiting for the poet to drop another clanger. When Elena was present the poet would smile: 'Go and make him a cup of tea. The man is working!'

The young man did not come for several days, and then an ambulance arrived and some men in white coats carried Michael away after a police doctor had spoken a few words to him, waited for a reply, received none, and pronounced him insane. Elena, who was fortunately there at the time, packed his bag and also managed to get the doctor into a corner. Embarrassed, glancing away, the doctor said he was clearly schizophrenic, but he would receive treatment and every care at such-and-such mental hospital (mentioning a name that made Elena blench).

The next day, Elena was sacked. In a fit of high spirit she had mistyped 1000 gross of mittens as 1000 gross of kittens – and even the stupid production chiefs had smelt a rat. She was sent to the very highest official in the Ministry. She asked to be allowed to speak to him in private. The official sent away his minions. As a result of what Elena said to him, the official promised that, although he could not rescind her dismissal for such a stupid error, he would see if he could (in return for certain favours) use his influence to have her friend moved to a sanatorium, where he would be treated simply as a re-cuperative case of nervous exhaustion. Elena thanked the official in the manner expected, and believed it a worthy sacrifice. A week or so later she received a postcard from Michael saying he had been sent on to a sanatorium by the sea, twenty miles from the city, and was being well treated.

Chapter Nineteen

To Elena, on a grubby New Year's card: 'Sleep & quietness. Walks along the cliff. Christmas day: washed my hair and listened to Mozart. Eyes better – I can see far off but not yet close. Thank you for your gift. Love, Michael.'

It might be quiet at the sanatorium, but in the city there was serious unrest. Crowds demonstrated peacefully, and were shot down. Roses bloomed in the snow – it was a time of blizzards. Government proclamations were defaced. The prison queues, it was said, were long. Explosions occurred. Gaps appeared in streets overnight. A leading official was assassinated. One day the Ministry building in which Elena had worked all but disappeared, with (it was rumoured) hundreds of deaths, though the authorities denied this. Newspapers came out spasmodically. One day they would show pictures of five or six traitors – yesterday's trusted leaders – with villainous close-crop-ped heads, and the leading article would demand summary punishment. At the same time, five or six smiling and obviously trustworthy faces would appear, elevated to the highest rank and given the city's highest honours. A week later, these same men, but with villainous close-cropped heads, would be denounced as traitors, and the leading article would demand summary, etc. Elena, like everyone with any sense, gave up buying the newspaper or turning on the radio. She kept indoors. She had no money to buy anything even if there had been anything to buy; the little she had managed to save from her typing job was swallowed up in rent. She existed by scrounging an egg here, a tin of soup there.

The house bulged at the seams with soldiers and refugee relatives. There was scarcely a room which did not contain at least one extra person. Michael's room had been taken over by soldiers, two of whom had lived there before, in different uniforms. They knocked on Elena's door and insisted she join them for a drink, just when she was mustering courage to knock on theirs and ask if she could take away her friend's books. She found his room already in a fearful state, though his books had not been touched. But Peter's mural had been defaced: they had disgracefully drawn obscene additions. They laughed when she gave them the edge of her tongue, and grabbed hold of her. She had to kick and struggle to get out safe and sound, to their jeering laughter.

Later, one of the nicer ones came to apologize for his friends. She shared some tea with him and they chatted about the critical situation. The young cadet officer, hardly out of school, said it was a great thing. Two days ago he had helped the common people break into the prison where Elena had 'stayed', and loosed the prisoners. This was the true victory for the people, he said, the end of tyranny.

But so had every changeabout been the true victory for the people, Elena thought. And if there was to be no more tyranny, why did she lie awake at night, as feet trampled the stairs and doors were hammered?

At last the permit she had been awaiting for months came through, granting her permission to travel outside the city to see the poet. She had not heard from him since the New Year's card, and she was anxious.

She put on her only decent dress, a plain but becoming white, and took from her work basket a sum of money she had put by from selling her sewing machine. It was a pleasant, mild day in early spring, and she enjoyed the fresh morning breeze as she set out for the station.

She could not resist smiling when she saw the posters at the corner of the street. Some said 'Forward!' While others said 'To the left!', which reminded her of the dancing classes in the old days. But when she had turned the corner she was struck by the altered appearance of her city, and it upset her. In all the human ugliness of these times, the city's beauty had remained constant. Now this too was growing ugly. It was not so much the half-destroyed buildings, for these could be rebuilt: it was rather the new buildings, totally without grace and in the wrong places. As the train, crammed with sailors and refugees, pulled out of the station and rounded the lagoon, she saw there were half-finished factory buildings even on the island that was always such a jewel, so green and peaceful. Now these ugly concrete buildings. She had tried to stop such monstrosities; instead of '10 new factories' she had typed 'no new factories'; but after the scandal over the kittens they had obviously checked her memos thoroughly.

Rounding the gulf, hugging the coastline, the train ran out of buildings and she began to enjoy the space beyond the dirty window. When, after an hour, the train stopped at a tiny station, she struggled out over the drowsing sailors' legs and kitbags.

Climbing the steep path to the sanatorium, she gulped the pure, cold wind from the gulf, gratefully. The sky was blue, except for a few puffy white clouds; the sun struck through the tops of the pine trees. She grew warm from climbing in the sharp cold, and took off her motheaten fur coat. There were snowdrops peeping up through the melting snow, and she bent to pick a bunch. Cresting the stony rise, she saw a man sitting on a garden seat, hunched in an overcoat, and she recognized Michael.

The poet was never to forget the sight of his friend, manifested suddenly through the pines, her white dress, the familiar fur coat on one arm, a bunch of flowers clutched in her other hand, the familiar warm delighted smile as she caught sight of him. The blue and spacious gulf in the background; snow and black pines. So she had not abandoned him! (Their letters and cards lay abandoned in various shunting yards.) He was to capture this manifestation in one simple, fresh lyric after another, all different yet all the same, in which Elena and the trees, the rocks, the snow and the sea were blended.

He had seen her in a dream, he told her, just the previous night, smiling at him and pushing her hair back from her eyes in just this way.

And partly, as she climbed the hill, she had reminded him of his sister. Now he confessed to her that the friend he mourned so much, the girl who had jumped from a window, had been more than a friend, had been his half-sister. He had hidden it because . . . 'That wasn't the only lie I told you,' he said, looking at her intently with his clear eyes.

He did not wish to speak about the days he had spent in the mental asylum. Only that the drugs he received gave him terrible hallucinations: a leopard springing at him out of a black forest, a scarlet rose from which crawled, endlessly, fat garden worms.

Chapter Twenty

The kindly doctor said Michael was well enough to go home, now that he had someone to keep an eye on him. They packed his case, he said goodbye to the nurses and fellow patients, and Elena and he returned together to the city, where snow was falling thickly and people were staggering to keep their feet.

He was shocked, but curiously elated, at the changes that had taken place. He seemed to feel that this genuinely represented a new beginning. Only the factories disturbed him; but even so, people had to be given work. Dignity, human dignity – which meant work for your hands – must come before beauty, or rather it *was* beauty. Persephone, wearing a cheap but cheerful scarf, was setting out from the shadows, purposefully, for the factory loom. 'My doctor has forbidden me depression . . .' dates from this time; while the poem 'In me are people without names,/Children, stay-at-homes, trees . . .', with its vivid evocation of the city's warm, homely, democratic bustle, probably relates to this period in the poet's life, though not written until much later.

Elena left him asleep on her bed – he was quite exhausted by the journey – begged some food from her friends, told them the good news, and took a little of the food up to the janitor. Spooning egg-white into his flaccid mouth, she told him she urgently needed a mattress and some blankets. A lawyer and his wife had 'gone' during the night, and the old man mumbled that she was welcome to take what she needed, before someone else moved in. Elena felt guilty, lugging the mattress down the stairs, but the living must come first. If the married couple ever returned, she would let them have their things back.

She placed the mattress on the floor near the oil stove, and rigged up some string across the ceiling and hung one of the blankets over it, splitting the room in half.

Neither of them had particularly noticed a commonplace man in the hallway when they arrived at the house, but he had spotted *them* and hurried to phone his editor. And in the morning, Peter came rushing to her room, brandishing a newspaper. On an inside page was a small out-of-date photo of the poet, and a short comment saying that readers would be glad to know of his recovered health and return to the city. It made brief reference to 'his great popular success, the *Snow Queen*, due for revival soon at the Arts Theatre'. The poet could not believe his eyes; but it was true enough, for an hour or so later his friend the director called, engulfed him in a bear hug, and invited him to the rehearsals. The play was due to open on the first of April, seven days from now. He was also authorized, said the director, to invite him to give a gala poetry reading.

There followed a week of frantic hustle at the theatre as Michael and his director friend worked the author's late thoughts into the production. It amounted to virtually a new play. The actors despaired of learning their new lines, and ranted as actors will. But they began to see the rightness and beauty of the changes; and on the first night, despite some rough passages, everyone was left feeling drained but uplifted. It was both more tragic and more joyous. In the final scene, where the ageing woman, the Snow Queen, recognizes and is recognized by her long-lost daughter, there was not a dry eye in the theatre.

Or so the starry-eyed widows, besieging Michael at the party afterwards, assured him; though the drunk and delirious director shattered their cliché and shocked their rouge by substituting 'cunt' for 'eye'. It seemed in his wine that he spoke truth: all sorts of respectable women pressed against the poet with scarcely muted suggestions. Strong poetry, it seemed, meant a strong aphrodisiac. Elena kidded him it was only the aftershave the director had given him. There were more flagrant propositions after his highly successful poetry reading before a youthful and high-spirited audience (they swarmed on to the stage and half-killed him in their enthusiasm for 'The people are the city . . .'). The young woman from Elena's office, up whose skirt he had barked, now brushed against him excitedly along with the other naïve and breathless questioners. He had to escape by pretending to need another drink, and was buttonholed by a middle-aged lady who reproved him, coquettishly, for writing such 'shocking' poetry. In the toilet, he pulled out of his pocket a pair of frilly white briefs, with a phone number written in lipstick.

But underneath all this flattering tomfoolery, he was moved by the way poetry had shown itself capable of surviving; he liked the look in these young students' eyes; poetry had been alive all the time, as the water had kept moving under the frozen river. The only slight worry was the paroxysm of coughing that had seized him at the start of his reading. He had never quite shaken off the cold he had caught while walking in the hills behind the sanatorium in a semi-blizzard. It seemed to be getting worse: he felt flushed; he felt terribly afraid of the disease which had killed several members of his family. But maybe he was just smoking too much. He must really be getting home. No, he could manage to walk, perfectly well. Why was everyone suddenly so concerned?

Tossing in his bed, he was preparing to fight a duel over Elena. He had taken the gun from his second, and was crunching through deep snow under pine trees, ready to turn and fire. As he walked, his boots sank deeper into the snow, till he was wading through it with great difficulty. (The sporadic gunfire outside the house presumably created this vision.) Dimly he saw Elena undressing, in the gap of the half-drawn blanket. The swaying of her hair, as she bent to take off a shoe, mixed with rain falling against the window; and that watery rain became the liquid she was forcing between his lips, which he coughed up again, with phlegm and blood. He had a vision of his mother. She had come home unexpectedly, and he was clapping his hands for joy; she had never looked so lovely, there were roses in her cheeks. But the roses were fading, she was coughing in his throat, she was struggling to breathe on his pillow, and she was lying very still in her pale coffin, while he was trying to revive her with soup and warm milk.

He was holding on to the snow queen, riding through the air. She was taking him somewhere to abandon him. The more she cried, over her shoulder, that she would look after him, the more certain he was that she would leave him. They skimmed over the lagoon, she switched directions swiftly and he was falling into the water, and beneath the water. He was choking, gasping for breath. He rose to the surface and gulped a deep breath – and there staring into his face was the bright full moon, who turned into Elena, looking down at him with blank indifferent eyes that all the same expressed unquenchable love. He went down in the water again, feeling the dreadful weight of it crush his breast. The weight slid to his legs and he could breathe again. He saw the darkness of Elena's room, heard the patter of sleet on the window, and was infinitely glad he had been dreaming. But the huge weight was still on his legs. He looked towards the foot of the bed and saw, with a strange calm, that a snake was coiled there, resting on his legs, a snake of bright colours that sparkled in the darkness. He sweated and lay still, terrified now. He could see the beady eyes of the snake watching him. If the bright coil moved towards him, he would die; but if it slid away, he would also die. He summoned breath to cry out to Elena, asleep on the mattress, but then he realized that the snake *was* Elena.

Chapter Twenty-One

In the intervals when he was not delirious, the colour of the blood he coughed told him to expect death: for he had been trained as a doctor. When Peter relieved Elena at his bedside he brought with him his sketch pad, and drew what he was sure would be the poet's death mask. A lock of hair glued to the forehead with sweat, the thin exhausted face, lifted, gasping for breath, as though he lived on a planet without oxygen.

The first bird of dawn was singing, cool and unhurried; and in Elena's pleasant dream he was an oboist, tuning in the orchestra yet at the same time starting the symphony with a cool unhurried solo. A shout from the audience broke the melody and she woke to Michael calling for her. She gave him a drink of water and sat beside him for an hour, as he wanted to talk. He insisted that he was dying only because she had never given herself to him. If she slept with him, he would be saved. His eye glittered feverishly but his forehead was cool. At that moment the girl would willingly and gladly have done anything for him; to sleep with him would have been a small matter. But of course, in his present condition, it was out of the question, and gently she told him so. If he would only wait till he was better, all things would be possible. He still argued that he would not get better *unless* she slept with him. He was growing agitated, sweating, and had a coughing fit. She gave him another drink of water, lay down in her cotton nightdress beside him and let him hold her. She whispered to him, lovingly, and soothed him asleep.

He spoke of his conviction to Peter: if she would sleep with him he would get well. She would not, so he would die. He gripped Peter's arm and demanded the answer to this conundrum: he would not get better till he slept with her and she would not sleep with him till he got better ... He felt desperate not because of death itself but because he was sure his poetry would not be allowed to survive his death. They would come and burn his books and papers. This was as irrational an obsession as the other. In fact, the authorities were showing great concern. Michael's editor, affable again and anxious, paid them a visit and brought two extra ration cards so that the poet would have the best of food. He arranged for the best doctor to call. He promised a Collected Works – before the project had even been discussed by the committee – hoping it would cheer him up. But still the poet was sunk in bitterness and despondency. He looked at Elena with hate.

In reality, Michael was getting stronger all the time that he believed he was getting weaker. Elena spent hours in queues, buying him luxuries such as the fresh bread rolls he loved with butter; and lay down with the sick young man, wanting him to draw life and warmth from her body. But the only thing he craved, she could not give, fearing to make him worse.

One afternoon when he was lying asleep, with the girl beyond the curtain, he had a curious, bright dream. He was on board a ship, sailing out through the gulf for warmer climes. Peter was with him, taking care of him, and among the other passengers was a girl who was the image of Elena. This girl was also in the last stages of consumption; her face thin and pale, her form wasted, her hand always at her mouth, suppressing a cough. They saw each other at a distance, on deck, and watched each other, but never spoke. The poet noticed that whenever he felt a little better, revived by the sea breezes, the girl would be worse, slumped in a deck chair, swathed in blankets, coughing continually into a handkerchief; or her anxious mother would say that she was lying down in her cabin, not well enough to come on deck. And whenever the poet felt worse, coughing his lungs up, slumped in a deck chair or resting in his cabin, the girl was up and about, quite lively and cheerful, even able to join in the game of quoits. Somehow, in his dream, he had to break the vicious circle. So, when her mother said sadly that the girl was lying down in her cabin, quite ill, he asked the waiter to give him some blancmange, and he took it down to her. He lifted the poor coughing girl so that she could eat the blancmange. At first it made her cough blood but gradually she began to take an interest in the food, and a natural colour came back into her cheeks. When she had eaten it all, to the last spoonful, they talked and joked, and both of them felt perfectly well. He got under the blanket and made love to her. Her mother came into the cabin unexpectedly, but was so overjoyed to see her daughter fit and well that she readily forgave the poet. The girl and the poet were married by the ship's captain.

He did not tell Elena about his dream, only his friend the painter. It so moved the good-natured young artist that when Elena came back from shopping he went immediately to his studio and tried to express the honeymoon voyage in oils. He painted a black ship, in a sea and sky that was one golden honey-glow of light. He stepped back from the canvas astonished at his own vision, for it was the first true painting he had been able to do for a very long time. He forgot all about Michael in the joy of his painting.

Now Michael was recovering day by day, and even *he* knew it. She would gladly have slept with him now, but he was no longer in such a painful fever of desire – perhaps he had already consummated it. But he relished the tasty fresh rolls with thick melting butter. Elena felt such a lightness of heart that she would have thrown the window open and flown into the April blue, or at least to the branches of the maple tree she loved so much.

Day by day it grew warmer. Every morning the poet would sit under a tree in the spacious, overgrown garden of the old palace, reading or writing. He felt almost glad to be weak, finding his dreamy convalescence very good for allowing images to drift up from his unconscious. Among others, the memory of Elena-as-moon, looking down at him with serene indifference, came back to him. The garden was secluded by high walls, and ran down to a line of trees, beyond which was the canal. The sun seemed to move more slowly across the sky. Peter, too, would bring his easel out sometimes, and paint the garden. The mood of that spring is caught in his painting of the line of trees, turbulent cumulus quietly massed without threat, a glimmer of still water through the elms, tall grass in the foreground; a painting that breathes stillness and languor – all except a small splash of red, under the elms, that is Elena's skirt.

The affable editor came and discussed the planned collected volume. But Michael found it hard to interest himself in earlier work – he was too busy writing the truly important works. These poems were so heavy with earth they could have been weighed in the greengrocer's scales. They were so earthy that even Psyche, the soul, was described as fond of trinkets, being feminine (he had given Elena a bracelet, a keepsake from his mother, and been surprised by her pleasure).

There were two afternoons he was never to forget, warm spring afternoons when they were on their own.

On the first day of May the clouds jostled slowly in the blue sky like ice floes, but in the garden it was breathless and hot. They lay stretched under the still elms. Her hand lay open in the long grass; he studied her fingertips and the criss-cross patterns left by stems in her palm. He breathed in the scents of the earth, scents of grass, may blossom, buttercups and cow-parsley; watched the ladybird creeping over her white blouse, the blue dragonfly hovering, the minute winged creature without a name settle on her forehead near the wisp of hair; watched her eyes to see how long it would be before they opened, conscious of his watching. When they opened they looked at him sleepily, peacefully, and closed again. Her hand strayed to her forehead to brush away the ephemerid but it had gone. He put his hand on her navy skirt and it was hot, soaking in the sun. He watched her moisten her lips with her tongue, then lapse back into stillness again. He pressed his elbows into the grass and couldn't believe so much beauty had been given to him.

Time could be weighed and the silence could be seen. He closed his eyes and knew that all this blessing still existed, and it would go on existing when he was dead, and he would still own it. He opened his eyes, and there was the dragonfly, the faintly rustling grass, the cow-parsley in the hedge. Death was an absurdity.

The second afternoon, two weeks later, was even more astonishing. He relived the experience of first love. They walked up to one of the hills to have a picnic. Whether it was that the picnic bag reminded him of a schoolgirl's satchel. Or whether it was the sudden unplaceable scent that transported him instantly to a country lane. Whether it was the three freckles on her thin white neck. Or whether it was that he felt light and unburdened, because a beggar had come up to him and he had given him – not having any coins in his pocket – his only coat (for one should always give to beggars). Whatever the reason, Elena, lying by him on the hill, looked like a girl and he had the feelings of a boy. A breeze caught the edge of her collar and fluttered her hair against his cheek, and at that moment some bright and painfully sweet thing formed in the base of his throat, flowed up into his mouth and to his eyes, touching the lashes with wet, and then flowed down through his body. He touched his lips to her hair and she turned her face into that touch, just brushing his lips with hers, because there were people trekking past with rucksacks. When she put her hand in his, that bright, painfully sweet substance reappeared at his nape and trickled down through his spine.

These were the times when she, too, felt so happy that she would gladly have given herself to him, even with the risk of people seeing them from the house or stumbling upon their dell. But she sensed that his mood was otherwise.

He wrote a poem about a woman of the streets who finds herself pregnant. Then he wrote a poem about a star, which made him unhappy and disturbed. He knew, whenever he wrote about stars, that he was about to come to the end of a cycle and could expect a drought, for the subject was leading him away from earth.

Chapter Twenty-Two

It was April again – but how changed from that other April . . . One evening in early summer the doctor who had attended him in his illness had turned up unexpectedly, sat with them hour after hour, licking his dry lips nervously and chain-smoking (as Elena saw in retrospect). They were both yawning but not wanting to be rude to their new friend. After the cathedral bell had tolled one, a hammering at the door; four black-coated men strode in like pall bearers, the acting janitor white faced and goggle eyed behind them. The police agents went smoothly into their routine, turning the room upside down, reassuring Michael that he would not need to take anything with him – he would soon be back – while Elena tried to stop shaking, for his sake, and the doctor scuttled out, his watching brief completed.

This was the most stupefied of all the partings he was later to analyse ('I have studied the science of goodbyes,/bareheaded laments in the night . . .'). He had a nightmare in which Elena, in nurse's uniform (or it might have been his mother), was cleaning him up, laying him out. He struggled to move, screaming that he was not dead, but no sound came from his lips. He thought it was a nightmare, in the instant of being shaken awake; but as he looked into the dazzling light he would have given anything to have returned to it. He had nothing to give ('There's no longer enough of me left for myself . . .').

In the morning when, shocked, she sat looking out of the window, Peter came rushing up with a newspaper. Clearly it explained why they had arrested him, and it could hardly have been worse. There was a letter, signed by twelve 'poets and citizens', denouncing the criminally seditious poem that had appeared in the leading literary journal – Michael's 'Gretchen and Dr Frankenstein'. It appeared that the poem was a brazen attempt to destroy the new, progressive, economic humanism (Dr Frankenstein) in the name of an archaic concept of imagination or idealism (Gretchen). Read by the young and the politically naïve, the poem could undermine their faith in the economic and social fabric, created by the people's sacrifice and courageous struggle against the forces of reaction, etc. As if that wasn't enough, the poem erred in other respects. Since it so obviously and crudely set up Gretchen, a fallen woman, as an object of admiration, even of reverence, it was 'morally putrid', a reversion to their talented colleague's earlier pornographic style which they had hoped he had outgrown. But even worse, the character of the monstrous Dr Frankenstein was clearly meant to suggest, to the reader, the city's most revered statesman. This wicked intention stood out a mile, from the poet's choice of descriptive phrases. Without question the author's work should be – by a droll misprint – 'prescribed', until he changed his ideas.

As 'Gretchen and Dr Frankenstein' contains only one descriptive term relating to the doctor – the image of the vulture – the letter writers were themselves walking on a marsh, and were soon to pay the price for their own naïve stupidity. Not that this was any help to Michael. His friends were filled with a sick fear as to what would happen to him. To have signed his own death warrant, in only sixteen lines of verse . . . And surely it *was* his death warrant, his ticket for the ferry (and perhaps the editor's too). At best, the poet might be sent to one of the camps that, according to rumour, were being set up in remote areas. A death sentence still, only more long drawn out.

Elena queued at the prison ('I come here as if it were home,' she said sadly to another woman in the queue), but was turned away at the door. She had next visited the high-ranking official who had helped her before, 'for a consideration'. Again she had found him sympathetic. He had pulled strings and managed to get Michael's sentence commuted to a term of exile in a provincial city. Elena had begged to be allowed to go with him, but that was no part of the bargain. Two evenings a week, a sleek sedan with a uniformed chauffeur would draw up outside the house, and Elena would step into it. She dreaded these occcasions, as the official had peculiar and unpleasant tastes. Then one evening the sedan had not come. She found that the high-ranking official had vanished. Instead of feeling relieved, she was terrified that they would remember the poet. She wrote to him at once, begging him, in veiled terms, to be careful and to keep a low profile.

Elena had endured, not for the first nor the last time in her life, a spell of clinical starvation. She survived on black bread and tea, by selling a few trinkets that the official had given her, and even her shabby old fur coat. There was no work to be had; especially for a woman who had 'Prostitute' and 'Wife of a convicted criminal' stamped on her pass book (they refused to accept that she had lived with the poet purely through love and compassion). She spent her time in bed – to save on heating – or in bread queues. There were queues for everything; the city teemed with starving, frozen, homeless people. Some of these were refugees from other parts, but most were peasants, driven to look for work here because of the run-down of agriculture in favour of rapid industrial growth. The old, the feckless, or simply the unlucky, could not find jobs, and slept on the river embankment or in ditches, continually harassed by the police. A new slang term came into being, for people who 'died on the move'. And every day, the railway station disgorged fresh masses of homeless.

Even the lucky ones who found jobs in the new factories were scarcely any better off. Everything was in short supply and out of the reach of their pockets. Scarcely anyone, for example, had a decent pair of boots; the authorities had still not caught up with Elena's deliberate mistake. True, a shoe factory had been built where the park used to be; but it was found that the machinery was only capable of producing boots and shoes for the left foot. According to the press and the radio, great strides were being made.

Elena wished she had been born a boy, and given a good trade by her parents. There was plenty of work for skilled tradesmen: builders, plasterers, painters, plumbers, carpenters and electricians. Areas of the city near the new factories were designated for cheap housing; architects competed for a prize to be awarded to the cheapest unit capable of being mass produced swiftly. Rows and rows of these prefabricated units were going up. Nothing worked in them, but at least the factory workers had a roof over their heads.

Away from the factories, some of the old houses were being restored and renovated. For several weeks Elena's walls and windows rattled with the noise of drills as the main wing of the former palace, with its superb outlook on the river, was returned to something like its former glory. As a result of this, many old faces were missing; it was said that they were being rehoused in a very nice new block of flats. When the work was finished, the result was a number of quite splendid apartments, each with five or six ample rooms. There was a day when the street was jammed with furniture vans and sleek black cars, and the stairs resounded non stop with the thump of furniture and the curses of carriers.

That very evening, after the dust had settled, there was a knock on

Elena's door. Opening it cautiously, she found her second husband standing there. She was taken aback, and flushed crimson with guilt because she had sold his wedding ring only three days before. How had he found out? But he greeted her very politely and asked if he might come in for a few minutes. He perched on the edge of a chair, and looked thoroughly out of place – nattily dressed from polished toecaps to starched collar. Refusing tea, he stared at Elena. In spite of her thin, careworn appearance and shabby dress, she was still beautiful. He cleared his throat and explained that he and his new wife had moved into one of the renovated apartments. He had done very well for himself, he was pleased to say – was now an assistant to one of the officials in charge of supplies. He had wanted to find out if she was still here. He was not a man to bear grudges. He could see she had paid for her sin. After ten minutes of such stiff conversation, he had gone. She breathed a sigh of relief that he hadn't mentioned the wedding ring.

A week later, and just before Christmas, all the remaining single-room tenants of the house received a cyclostyled letter demanding full payment of outstanding rents – Elena owed money for the past three months – and doubling all rents for the next quarter. As an alternative, it suggested, tenants might be prepared to 'double up' by sharing their accommodation with one of the city's homeless. As well as being to their financial advantage, it would be a seasonal act of charity on their part. If they were prepared to go further, 'double up' again, the authorities might be prepared to be magnanimous and write off existing debts. In return, they must be prepared to serve the community by carrying out household duties for the occupants of the new apartments, all of whom (as they knew) were engaged in exhausting and vitally important work. They would receive food and clothing in return for their services. At a time of high unemployment, the letter continued, they would recognize this opportunity for what it was, a stroke of great good fortune. In lieu of their accepting this generous offer, one month's notice would be given. The letter concluded by wishing all tenants a merry Christmas and happiness for the New Year.

Elena had to read the letter several times before she understood what it was getting at. She wondered what to do. She would have asked Michael, or Peter – but her artist friends had made themselves scarce long ago, in the general tightening-up that had followed the letter from the twelve 'poets and citizens'. She had nowhere to turn. She would never get another room. A quarter of a room was better than nothing. She would rather go on the streets than skivvy for the sleek fat faces who pushed by her on the stairs; but what is a prostitute without a room and a bed? Besides, she had heard the police were vigilant at whipping the whores off the streets and into prison.

And so, this April, by a complicated system of mattresses and sleeping bags, strings and blankets, she was sharing her room with a homesick girl from the country, and two gentle old ladies, sisters, who had known better times. The room stank – the country girl did not wash very often – but they were only in it to sleep. By day they worked in the official apartments, cooking, cleaning, looking after children. Elena worked for her second husband – he had called again and asked her personally to work for him. The homesick country girl worked in his apartment too. In her loneliness she had started to cling to Elena, who felt sorry for her in spite of her smell, and Elena persuaded her ex-husband to employ her. He was at least not an unkind man. 'Better the devil you know than the devil you don't know.'

The day began at seven-thirty – cleaning up from the night before, and preparing breakfast. It ended at nine in the evening, after they had served dinner and taken part in family prayers: he was still very pious. Most days they had a couple of hours off in the afternoon; but they could never be sure of it. The devil Elena had *not* known, the mistress, proved strict and capricious. She was unattractive and getting on in years; widowed previously, and bringing to the marriage a crippled and mentally backward girl of seven. The child was still in nappies; looking after her needs and tantrums was an exhausting day's work in itself. For all its spaciousness, the apartment felt more claustrophobic than her own little quarter of a room: stuffy, like the stuffed animals' heads on the walls; trapped and gloomy, like the dark-green potted plants. And every inch of the heavy angular furniture had to be wiped and polished twice a day, under the eye of the ugly implacable mistress.

Chapter Twenty-Three

He certainly could not have married her for love, Elena decided. More probably for money and influence: the wife carried herself like someone used to having her every whim obeyed. She would spend ages planning the menu for a dinner party, and went into a rage if her plans were thwarted — such as the occasion when Elena went to the special shop reserved for officials and came home without the tin of green figs because there was a temporary shortage. The mistress threw a casserole dish against the wall, and cried with vexation. Elena, indeed, wondered if she was slightly mad, since her reactions were so unpredictable and disproportionate. Also she treated her poor daughter very badly, even to lock her away in a dark cupboard. No wonder the poor child was sickly and backward: she was frightened out of her wits.

She could see that her employer was unhappy, from the way he looked at his wife across the dinner-table . . . as though sizing up a Zulu chief. She thought he looked at *her*, sometimes, regretfully. He talked to her in private about his stepdaughter. He was worried about the way his wife behaved to her; he admitted as much to Elena. He said he would like her to take sole charge of the child, try to train her up properly and teach her things. It would be something if she could at least sign a cheque when she grew up.

So Elena took charge of the girl, and did her best to help her, with kindness and firmness. It was not easy. But she felt triumphant when the girl learned to use the toilet. Predictably, the little girl's mother did not like this development one bit, feeling her authority to be slipping. But her husband insisted. And Elena was to be treated properly. She was to have her own bedroom in the apartment, keep civilized hours, not have any more skivvying to do. She must take her meals with them too, both because she was a lady and so that she could guide the child's table manners. Looking after the girl was such a thankless and wearisome task that she must be given a little dignity.

She could see his wife's eyes burning into hers, every time she sipped from her cup. Though her employer had given her money to buy a smart dress at the special shop, she was careful to buy it in a sober brown shade and to keep it simple. She knew better than to set up as a rival. She kept to her place, and fell into bed dead to the world after coping with the unruly girl all day. The child was beginning to know her letters; Elena could smile with satisfaction at a job well done, each night as she closed her eyes. Virtue was its own reward; and as a bonus — her old problem, insomnia, was a thing of the past!

Though sometimes she woke up with a jolt, after a sensation of falling. No wonder: she walked a tightrope, between the child's whims, and her employer's, and his wife's. A couple of times she had had to fend off her employer's fumbling hands, and then look as if nothing had happened, when his wife entered the room. But he had apologized, very nicely, and bought her a box of chocolate mints. She felt a bit sorry for him — she couldn't imagine his wife giving him much pleasure in bed.

One night she was shaken awake, and looked up into his alarming face. There had been a near-tragedy. His wife, after a quarrel with him in the bedroom, had tried to set fire to herself. Fortunately her nightdress did not burn easily and he had managed to beat out the flames. But she seemed to be in shock. He didn't know what to do. Elena got out quickly and went to the unconscious woman. Her legs looked quite badly burnt. And he had not even rung for the ambulance! He must do so at once. The child was crying. Elena went to reassure her, told her a little story, and she was asleep again before the ambulance men arrived. The woman was laid on the stretcher, and her husband, wearing a kind of sleepwalking look, put on his hat and coat and followed them downstairs.

The injuries were more serious than they had thought. Her stomach, too, was badly burnt. There would have to be skin grafts. She would be in hospital for months.

Elena capably took charge of the apartment, even to being hostess at an important dinner party. She made sure the rooms were aired, and even persuaded the servant to have a bath now and then. She was kind to the girl, made sure she had plenty of time off, and bought her some smart clothes to boost her morale. She was really quite an attractive, lively girl, now that she washed — and smiled. When they were alone in the apartment, Elena treated her more as a companion than a servant. They chatted and laughed together in the kitchen. Apart from the child, there was really very little work to do, if you were not too fussy.

A card came from the poet. He was well. Had she bottled the wine as she had promised? She wrote back that the wine was bottled. When he had been lying at death's door, convinced (rightly, as it happened) that the authorities would try to destroy his work, she had tried to cheer him up by promising to learn all his poems by heart. She had a good memory, and she had started to learn them there and then, even though many of them were double dutch to her. She had continued to memorize them after the police agents had removed the poet's books and papers, because she had duplicates hidden away in her work basket. Now she knew every one of them, from the first poem he would still own to – 'What would Troy be to you, men of Achaea, without Helen?' – to the most recent, 'the duelling of nightingales'. She had said them over and over to herself while she scrubbed and polished; and still said some of them to herself last thing at night and first thing in the morning. She was terribly afraid that one morning she would find she had forgotten her lines.

Elena, of course, knew that some of the love poems were about her, and learning these brought a spot of red to her cheeks. If, for one moment, she had known just how many had been inspired by her – *dictated* by her, he might have said – she would have been deeply uncomfortable. But the descriptions were so clearly not about her, most of the time – her hair, done up in a bun, was no 'downward-burning flame', for instance – that she simply wondered who this exquisite woman had been. She must ask him. It depressed her, rather – to think she was so ordinary and commonplace and weak, doing what was expected of her, taking the line of least resistance.

She had started sharing her employer's bed. It had seemed, after a time, the natural thing to do, since she shared everything else and was responsible for everything. She felt, in a way, it was her duty; since her first husband must be presumed dead, she could not escape the feeling that she was legally bound to this man. Strictly, they had never been divorced, and he now said that his conscience was troubled; he believed he had committed bigamy. It was not too late to ask forgiveness for his sin; but they must live truly as man and wife once more. So Elena consented. He was stiff and narrow, but she was quite fond of him. Also it put her in a stronger position to protect the child. The poor girl had started to masturbate, quite openly, because she didn't know it was wrong, and her stepfather took the strap to her. Elena made it a condition of their resumed marriage that he would treat the child more gently.

As regards 'that' side of their relationship, it was not working out well. In fact, it was much worse than before. He expected her not to move or show any feeling while he relieved himself into her. If she had an orgasm – and even in bad sex, orgasms will sometimes come – she had to lie still and stiff and quell the sensation. She began to wonder if *this* had caused the broken casserole dish and the burnt nightdress.

Chapter Twenty-Four

Once Elena had cooked breakfast for her husband and found some chores to occupy her 'help', she had the rest of the day to kill. She did not like walking in the city, it was so full of misery; and her favourite park had been swallowed up. Occasionally she went to the cinema, but there was always a 'clean family picture' on, which bored her stiff. She knitted clothes for a poor girl in the house who was expecting a baby – and she read the newspaper from end to end. And one day the obituary column carried the news of the death of the old janitor, in a certain geriatric hospital. The cremation was to be tomorrow.

She felt sad. She had done her best for him, until the time when only a hospital or a devoted daughter could cope. She had returned good for evil. But he had not been a bad old man, as old men went. He had seemed older than the house, and there had been a degree of security in knowing he was in charge. At least in his time nobody had more living space than anyone else. Even the rape she found more comic than anything else, now. He had had a bit life in him, which was more than could be said for her husband.

She shed a few tears. For a drunken, brutal, lecherous old man! Yet there were other reasons for her tears. She felt sorry about his death because she hated what had been done to the house. Hadn't it been the point of the revolution that people should be equal? Yet the more the authorities glorified equality, the more unequal people obviously were (the 'servants' now had to use a different entrance, at the back, in God's name!). The louder they shouted liberty, the more chains they threw around people; and the more they spouted of brotherhood, the more clearly was one's brother a wolf.

She lay under the stuffed heads and stroked herself to find out if she was still alive. She felt ungrateful. Others were infinitely worse off. Yet she would gladly have changed places with the pregnant girl who lived off the crusts from the kitchens where her room-mates worked. Better the rats under the floorboards than the stuffed heads and potted plants.

Events had isolated her. The sick little girl had suffered a recurrence of the masturbation problem. Her stepfather brought home – of all things – a pair of handcuffs. He beat her when she became incontinent again. It was best, in the child's interest, for Elena to go along with his plans to send her away to a special boarding school. Elena missed her, and sent her sweets every week. Her real mother could do nothing, even if she had wanted to, having gone straight from skin grafting to electric shock treatment.

Elena wanted a child of her own to fill the gap in her life; but there was no chance of that. Her husband spent most of his time at the office; usually he had to dash out again after dinner, and by the time he returned, Elena had drugged herself asleep. On the rare occasions when they spent some time together, he showed no interest in her, sexually. Knowing he admired slim-waisted women, she bought a rather chic boned corselet in the special shop, when some very nice imported underwear came in. But he was hardly around to see it, and, when he was, he averted his eyes as she undressed. The corselet reduced her sexual frustration, but only by making her feel faint.

She was even denied the cameraderie that had once existed with her 'help'. Elena had enjoyed her earthy country wit, her obscenities had cut through the repressive atmosphere. But lately she had been subdued by a harsh rebuke from her master for being familiar. Now she did her chores quickly and silently, and went back to her room.

Elena's sleeping pills didn't work any more. She lay awake, waiting for her husband. At one or two o'clock perhaps, he'd return from his office, exhausted – snoring almost before his head touched the pillow.

He was always respectful of her, especially in front of his colleagues and their wives, on the terrible evenings of the dinner parties; and he took her out driving on Sundays. Soon, he said, all his labour would reap its reward. When they increased their staff to cope with the rising supply problem, he'd move up the ladder, and they might even be able to have a house of their own, in one of the best areas. Perhaps even a cottage by the sea for weekends. And they'd be able to use, not just the special shop, but the *very* special shop reserved for the highest officials and their wives. Life was opening out.

Elena gave what she could to the poor; but for every hand that grasped the coins there were a hundred that stayed empty. She thought of running away, but where could she run? She worried about the poet, too, having had no word from him for several weeks. She checked in the only decent bookshop. There were plenty of modern poets she had never heard of; but not one of Michael's books. It was as she feared. In the Arts Encyclopedia (second edition) she found that his small inaccurate entry had been replaced by a brief definition of something called a tetrastich.

One day she was startled momentarily out of her lethargy by a confirmation in the newspaper of her first husband's death, 'of natural causes', in an unspecified place. There was a two-inch appreciation, saying that he had played a minor but meritorious role in the pre-revolutionary movements. And Elena hadn't even known! She felt – not sorrow, exactly, for one could hardly call it a marriage at all, it had been so brief and so peculiar. But sadness, yes; grief for herself. She grew conscious of the flight of time. She looked in the mirror, and was struck by the sternness of her face. Her hair pulled back sharply into a bun, the way her husband preferred it, she looked more like a spinster than a wife.

It was a Saturday, but there was nothing to look forward to. Her husband was away for the weekend on an official deputation somewhere or other. Even her help was away, on a visit to her family in the country. Elena remembered kneeling with her dead husband before the wooden crucifix. Someone had stolen the ruby, and she had burnt the wood in the stove, during the bad winter. She wanted to do something for his memory. She put on her hat and coat, and went out. She prayed for his soul in one of the few churches that remained open – even her husband had ceased to pray. When she called at the smart jewellers, looking for a crucifix to wear, they told her they were not being made any more. But at last she found one, in an antique shop in a poor district; a tiny silver cross on a silver chain. It was typical of Elena that she should wear such a thing just when everyone else was giving them up.

Chapter Twenty-Five

Luxury for the few and hunger for the many had become so much a matter of routine that the city appeared to run smoothly enough. The number of children who died 'on the move', that winter alone, would make interesting reading, but no figures exist. Perhaps the one good thing that could be said about that year was that the level of deliberate violence and terror had dropped. People no longer froze at the sound of a car approaching in the night. There was a newspaper correspondence about 'excessive zeal' having occurred in the past, involving acts of dubious legality.

Yet a more subtle, entirely legal, kind of violence was still present. This was brought home sharply to Elena when, just before Christmas, the two gentle old ladies who shared her former room with her 'help' were arrested for debt, and sentenced to a short term of imprisonment from which they would probably not emerge alive. Their employer had dismissed them from domestic service, a few months before, as being too old and infirm to work properly. They claimed he had promised to continue to pay their rent; he denied this. Elena wished they had told her they were in trouble, and she tried to pay their debts to the court; but for some reason this was illegal and the law had to take its course. But surely, thought Elena, the law existed to protect such people as these – two gentle, humdrum old ladies? She begged her husband to intercede with their former employer, who was quite a close friend; but he didn't see why he should interfere. It was simply life, he said: the fittest surviving and the weakest going to the wall. After a blazing row – which he brought to an end by striding back to the office, with a pained, long-suffering expression – she did not speak to him for a fortnight.

And then, unexpectedly, a most generous act of kindness on his part. The poet had turned up at her door, his term of exile over. That was not all – he brought a boy with him, a fine-featured, fair-skinned lad of nine, very quiet, serious and polite. Michael introduced him, a shade hesitatingly, as his nephew. The boy's grandmother had been looking after him, but now she was dying; on his way back from exile he had stopped off at his native town to collect the lad. Elena, naturally, made him welcome, made a fuss of him; she could see the family resemblance.

Michael himself was in a shocking state, dirty, ill (an unhealthy bluish tinge around the lips), and one would have said he was an old man. He had had a touch of heart trouble, he explained, though luckily no recurrence of the TB: the bitter climate of his place of exile had at least been good for that. Elena saw he had suffered far more than his guarded letters had implied. 'But I was grateful even for the heart attack,' he said. By rights he ought to have been in the grave like his brother. He'd seen it as extra time in a football match, and the whistle still hadn't blown! Elena cooked them a big supper; it was late and she had eaten her own dinner; her help had gone and her husband was out to a meeting. She was glad about that; she was afraid of what her husband would say when he found a 'convicted person' in his apartment, and she wanted to gather up her courage to face him. After they'd had their meal she gave the boy a good scrub in a hot bath, then ran it again for Michael. She turned out for him an old suit of her husband's, and said she would buy the boy a nice new suit in the morning. She tucked him in bed, and then sat with Michael in the lounge, sipping brandy. He mixed tender looks, unable to get over how beautiful she still was, with flashes of bitterness. It had shocked him when she wrote to say she was back with her husband.

She asked him about his nephew. He had never spoken of him before. He very rarely discussed his brother Joseph or anything to do with him; he felt his death too acutely. But he explained, now, that his brother had been married to a beautiful girl who had been killed tragically in an accident on the underground. He, Michael, had gone with his brother to identify her body. He had few more terrible memories. His shattered brother had taken the one-year-old baby to live with his wife's mother; and since Joseph's death she had been bringing him up alone.

Elena sighed, thinking it was the children who suffered most in these evil, violent times. What chance would they have of growing up to be decent happy people?

It made her all the more determined to be especially kind to the boy, and she was prepared to fight her husband if he cut up rough. She drank several whiskies.

Astonishingly, when her husband returned, just after midnight, he was geniality itself. He sipped an orange juice with them and questioned his wife's friend sympathetically on his painful experience. He insisted that Michael and the boy stay in the apartment – there was plenty of room – at least until his residence permit and work permit came through. Or maybe he would not have to find a job; he was pleased to hear the poet say he was writing a novel. On the whole novels were more acceptable, more positive and realistic, and it was not beyond the bounds of possibility that he would get his book published. He would have a word with someone. Elena wondered at how well they seemed to be getting on, chatting together. Her husband did not seem to mind the too obvious glances of tenderness and jealousy.

Warmed by his kind attitude, she tried to show her appreciation when they went to bed. But he was sleepy – and it was certainly true that he was being grossly overworked. Putting her arm round him as he prepared to sleep, she said he really must take it easier or he'd be having a heart attack too. He said sleepily that he couldn't ease up, there was so much that only he could do. He felt bad about leaving her on her own so often, and it would be nice for her to have Michael around for a while, it would be company. Maybe he was not such a bad man after all, she thought, listening to him snore; and she went to sleep with the thought of what colour suit she should get tomorrow for the boy.

There followed a happy time. They took the boy to the cinema and the zoo and the circus, to which he responded with solemn pleasure. Elena caught herself singing in the bath; having a lively poet around (for he had recovered his sparkle) made even her husband behave more genially. One dinner time their help spilled gravy on his trousers and all he said was, 'Accidents will happen.' He was greatly interested in the poet's novel. What was it about? Michael, who in private was consumed with guilt at writing prose, waxed warmly enthusiastic about it, and his cheeks flushed with the wine and knowledge of the characters coursing through his bloodstream. It was a poetic novel, he explained; it celebrated the tragic but beautiful countryside round the place of his exile, celebrated nature before it vanished in the night. Elena kicked him under the table, as she was still not totally sure of her husband's motives. 'Go on,' said her husband, fascinated. And, said the poet, it was about an ageing rake and a pure young man, father and son, and both in love with and tormented by the same beautiful but sadistic girl who was a prick teaser. Her husband blushed and dropped his gaze, and so did Elena. Absently and in embarrassment she stroked the bracelet Michael had given her.

Sometimes after dinner they would, all three, go to a concert, or they would do a little concert of their own, the husband at the piano, a rather wooden accompanist, and Elena and Michael attempting duets. Music had become more and more important to Michael, during his lonely exile. The old woman from whom he had rented a corner had an old gramophone and a few classical seventy-eights, which he had played over and over. Now to his surprise – and hers – he found that Elena had a very pleasant voice, while he could at least hold a descant, baritone or tenor as the mood took him.

More often, her husband would have to go out, leaving them listening to records, or just talking with a drink. In those long evenings, the boy safely tucked up in bed, she rediscovered the joy of his kisses. When her husband returned, he would usually go to bed, after a brief chat, and leave them still talking or listening. It was a painful delight to her, finding her body respond again, and a few times she went into the poet's bedroom and let him fondle her under her clothes. But she stopped him, always, before any real harm was done. She badly wanted him to make love to her, but she thought it would be unfair to her husband who was being so nice. Michael hated her for her cruelty, and hated her leaving him to go to her own bed – though she assured him that if he only *knew*, he would not be worried. Leaving him agitatedly smoking a cigarette, she half-thought that he was enjoying his agitation. She accused him once of being turned on by the unusual situation they were in, and he responded by accusing her even more angrily of being cruel and sadistic in reminding him that she belonged to someone else.

Chapter Twenty-Six

She turned water into wine and then removed the glass from his lips. He was wild for her impurities, asked her to do childish indecent things which she refused. He lay awake most of the night, excited, distraught, imagining Elena and her husband enjoying passionate love, for she was a born liar. He was waking her up, seeking her lips, stroking between her thighs ... He switched the light on, smoked cigarette after cigarette, wrote poems of passion much in excess of the facts ('Take your hand off my breast./We are high-tension cables ...' 'You fling your dress from you/As the coppice flings away its leaves ...'). He depicted himself as a sparrow, nestling in her enormous lap, under her gigantic breasts ('O vows, O perfumes, O infinite kisses!'). Elena too was lying awake, planning to leave her husband and go off with Michael as he begged, and never mind residence permits or work permits. What stopped her in her tracks was the belief that he was afraid of happiness, and therefore happier being unhappy. It hurt but did not surprise her to meet, on a scrap of paper, the phrase 'The passion to break away'.

Nor was Michael surprised when, after a leading article decrying 'pseudo-artistic forces opposed to industrialization', a letter came refusing him permission to live and work in the city. Astonishment was reserved for the last paragraph, which said that in recognition of his past service to literature the authorities were awarding him an old age pension. He would become the youngest old age pensioner in history! The weekly sum they mentioned would be just enough to keep him in cigarettes and matches.

He would go back to his native town, he said. There was no doctor within twenty miles and, although he was not properly qualified, he knew enough medicine to keep himself alive. 'An egg for a bottle of cough mixture and half a dozen for an appendix.' The town was beyond the proscribed radius, but not so far away that he could not visit the city once in a while, as he was permitted to do.

He asked Elena and her husband if they would take care of his nephew until he got himself somewhere to live. On his last night with them, she memorized his new poems, after which he struck a match and burnt them. 'There weren't any lice,' she said, smiling sadly – a reference to his verse comparing her sadistic purity to the way her nails had probed his nephew's hair for lice on the night of their arrival.

She held the boy's hand tight as they waved to the white face and outstretched arm. She wiped her eyes and gave the child the hanky to blow his nose.

She did her best to keep cheerful for his sake. They made again the round of zoo, circus and cinema. She did schoolwork with him, several hours a day, and found him a willing learner. He liked some of the pictures in the art books, so she took him to an exhibition which was receiving rave publicity; but they both found it dull and disappointing. To make up for that, she took him straight off to see a cartoon film, and bought him ice cream. They had good times together. She felt very fond of him. Then came a letter from Michael saying he had settled into a room, earned himself a few patients, and would she send his nephew to him by train.

It was a November of heavy mists. Afternoon by afternoon and evening by evening she would stand looking out of the window. Instead of the amber lights of the embankment and the bridge reflecting sharply on the wide river, they were a vague orange blur. Her husband had to work even longer hours. After the busy, happy weeks, she felt completely isolated and useless and bored. There were times when she might have shot herself, if she had had a gun. She contemplated opening the window and jumping, but she was afraid of heights, she thought it a dreadful death. She still tried hard with her husband, still put on fresh make-up and a fresh dress to be attractive when he came home for dinner; still choked in the figure-flattering corset. But almost before their help had served the coffee and gone, he was glancing at his watch and jumping up, taking a last gulp and dabbing his mouth with the napkin.

She lay on the sofa listening to records, dreaming of happier times and imagining that she was developing all sorts of complaints: Why had her heart fluttered? Why was she finding it difficult to breathe? What was that pain in her shoulderblade? Was that a lump in her breast?

One evening, mist piling against the window and cancer eating at her womb, she had the wild idea of asking her maid to go to the pictures. For once there was a film on that looked promising. She resented the way her husband insisted on keeping the servants in their place. It wasn't much fun for the girl either, going back to her cold and lonely room every night. Her husband would be back late and need never know.

She put on her coat and went down to the servants' quarters. She hadn't set foot in them since her husband found out that she was helping the pregnant girl. Yet she still felt more at home here. When she knocked on the door of her room – it was still, strangely, 'her' room – there was no reply. Disappointed, she was about to go away; but a noise inside the room arrested her. She put her ear to the door. The girl had gone out leaving the boiler on; there was a rhythmic thumping noise, quite loud and alarming. It was very careless of the girl; from the sound of it, it might explode at any second. There was a way of slipping the lock, which Elena had discovered on one occasion when she had gone out without her key. She tried it again now, and after a little effort it worked: she turned the knob and the door opened.

She stood in the doorway while her mind clicked as the lock had done. She saw the girl on the bed, her face buried in a pillow, her dress up round her back, her rump in the air, taking the thrust of Elena's husband. He still had his navy socks on. Rapt in the act of thrusting in and out, their backs to her, they were unaware of having a visitor. She walked quietly to the bed. Her husband caught sight of her out of the corner of his eye, gasped, and backed out. The girl's buried mouth gasped, 'Don't pull out! Fuck me harder! I'm nearly shitting myself!' and another remark Elena did not catch. Then the girl looked over her shoulder, and swivelled her body into a sitting position. Elena took a packet of cigarettes from her bag, and lit one to steady her nerves. The lovers stared at her, goggle eyed, running in sweat.

'Let's change rooms,' Elena said to the girl, softly.

The man made tea at Elena's suggestion, and watched bewildered as the two girls flitted to and fro, in and out of the room, with armfuls of clothes and other items. Elena noticed a lilac petticoat she'd admired months ago in the special shop. 'That's nice,' she said. The tenant next door, chauffeur to one of the rich families, came out of his room just as Elena arrived with a stack of dresses. He gave her scarcely a glance – such changeabouts were always happening. 'But I thought we were happy,' said the bewildered husband as Elena threw underclothes into a drawer. 'You don't understand! She's only a servant! It's because I respect you! I couldn't have done those things to you!' He smiled ineptly, and wondered if it was too late to run to the all-night kiosk to buy her the chocolate mints that she liked.

Chapter Twenty-Seven

Elena lived very quietly, gratefully relearning her room and the maple outside. She sold most of her clothes, and all of her jewellery except the bracelet and the silver crucifix. It made enough to pay the rent for a few months. She lived mostly on black bread and tea, and was quite happy. It disgusted her to look back at her rich living. And above all she would not accept any money from her husband. She considered herself divorced.

Again the blanket was up and she was sharing the room. It happened in this way: one morning there was a rather diffident knock on the door and she had opened it to a woman with a suitcase. She was neither very young nor particularly pretty, but of striking appearance: Elena took in the firm, sad, generous lips, the brilliant, large, glowing eyes, and the connection seemed so obvious that she said simply, 'You're alive!'

'I'm looking for my brother,' said the girl. 'Someone gave me this address.' Elena nodded, drew her inside, and explained that her brother was now living in his native town. The poetess – for it was she – said, 'You must be the girl in The Wedding Party!' Elena nodded, smiling.

Sitting at the table over a cup of tea, the poet's half-sister, Marion, told Elena about the 'lost' years since they had parted. ('You know about that?' she asked, and Elena nodded.) She had left Michael because she was in 'a chaos, a calvary' – she spoke breathlessly and in such elusive yet vivid terms that Elena found it hard to follow; as if the girl were not looking straight at her with those wide and sombre eyes but speaking to her from behind her shoulder. She had tried to disappear from the face of the earth, by teaching schoolchildren in a small town; but had cooked her goose by teaching them forbidden subjects. One of the schoolgirls had reported her for using the words 'soul' and 'immortality' – quite enough, with her 'morbid' and 'subjective' poems, to get her sent away for a very long time. Since it was not, then, illegal to speak of religious concepts, they had trumped up another charge, that of inducing her girl students to take part in sexual activities with her.

She knew of her reported death. It had certainly been in her mind to commit suicide. When she was put in a cell she had panicked, hammered on the door crying, 'Please, you must let me out – I wasn't made for prisons' – a terribly naïve thing to say. She had thought of jumping through the window – they left her unguarded in the interrogation room as though inviting her to do it – but in fact a brave girl who was in the next cell had jumped. Happening so soon after her arrest, Marion's friends assumed it was she. She could get no word to them. She was as good as dead anyway. More than once, the interrogator had grinned and clicked his fingers, the symbol for shooting.

But she believed that someone who liked her work and who had influence at the highest level had saved her life. Thinking she was going to be executed, she found herself dumped on a night train to a foreign capital, and told she was no longer a citizen and must never return.

She had lived a wandering, ghostly existence all these years. Sending letters to Michael and other relations but with no hope that they would get through. She had been terribly homesick and ill for a long time. She had had unhappy love affairs, usually with men who turned out to be married. So often, she said wryly, she had been 'the best friend of other women's husbands' – an expression she was to use again, later, in one of her poems, and that Elena was to recall as she learnt it by heart. She had been drawn to everything doomed; had undergone, and was still undergoing, a 'polar expiation' for the sins of her youth. She had heard news of Michael once or twice, and it was a joy to her when the comedy that she had mentioned was actually published in a pirated edition and she could read it. She revered his work – much more than he did hers. Every year or two she had written to the authorities saying she was contrite and begging to be allowed to return to her city. This last time, to her astonishment and joy, they had replied yes, on condition that she would stay within the city and report to the police every day. It was worth it, to come home. In her spirit she had never been away.

Elena felt drained when she had finished, and as though all her nerves had been twitched. The girl was much more intense, on the surface, than her brother; she thought if she touched her she would be electrocuted. They sat up talking all night. The girl cried, sometimes for happiness, sometimes for grief, while Elena told her about Michael; and she appeared especially upset and agitated when she heard he had brought his nephew to stay, and what a lovely child he was. She questioned Elena, wanting to know everything about him.

She hadn't known about her elder brother's death. She had got over her weeping spell; now she said that she had expected it. He was afraid of nothing and no one and was bound to find an early grave. She was glad the end had been swift, a bullet in the brain. He was a good person, she said, gazing through Elena. And so was his wife. They had done her a great kindness once. Her sister-in-law had been killed only a few days before her own arrest. 'It was a dreadful time – turmoil – turmoil' – and a nerve started twitching in her throat.

'I've died twice already,' she sighed, as they sat by the window and watched the dawn bring into creation the maple tree, the snowy street, a sliver of frozen canal. Marion recalled sitting at a window like this, in just such a room, when it had first come to her what she must do with her life. She had been reading some of Michael's earliest poems. She asked Elena to recite some more of her brother's later work, and she listened breathlessly, breaking into a smile that made her suddenly seem radiantly beautiful. It was poetry, she said; the real thing, that takes the top off your head.

All she had in the world was in her case. That did not bother her, she said; she had everything she needed. She felt equally indifferent to the loss of so much of her early, 'dissolute' poetry. It did not matter: it happens. The only thing that mattered was the next poem.

She must stay here, Elena insisted; she would write straight away to Michael and break the marvellous news. She made a point of preferring the mattress on the floor, and gave Marion her bed.

Quickly they became good friends. It was as if they had known each other all their lives. At times Elena could even see – mostly from the short, dark, pulled-back hair, and around the mouth – just why Michael had at first taken her for his half-sister. They were, really, not unlike. But Marion had this rare and all-possessing gift, while she had none. She was quite content to cook what little food she could scrounge, while her friend perched on her bed, the blanket pulled across, writing. She was a very private person; Elena would hardly see her to talk to for days, except for a brief word of thanks when she accepted food – fortunately she had a birdlike appetite – or in passing when she went out to report to the police. This was the only time she went out; she was completely happy in her half of a room.

The poems, when she gave them to Elena, begging her to memorize them in case of 'accidents', turned out to be love poems still, but of loss and jealousy, not joy. The only exceptions were poems about nature and about eternity, which she called 'the flood subject'. These, too, were love poems of a special kind. She asked her friend, anxiously, whether she thought the poems 'breathed'. Elena was doubtful; she found them even more difficult to understand than some of the brother's; but she said she liked them and she committed them to memory. She also 'gave' Marion her brother's poems from the time of their parting. One could not be too careful; indeed, it would be remarkable luck if even one of them survived to better times.

It was not as solemn as it sounds. Even when the girl was cooped up, behind the blanket, Elena felt in touch with her, sharing the excitement of writing at such white heat. And every few days, she would come out of isolation, decide it was time to let her hair down, change from her normal 'working' dress, a plain white cotton, to the only other frock she possessed, a red silk, and she and Elena would have a good long chat, till the early hours of the morning. Or they would take a walk along the canal bank, enjoying the night air free from the noise and fumes of traffic. The poetess had a rich sense of humour, despite everything that had happened. She could tell droll anecdotes that made Elena almost fall off her chair with laughing so much.

Elena also liked the way she would bring a thank-you gift: only a flower, or a sprig of lilac blossom that she had picked on her way back from the station; but she would place it reverently in Elena's hand as though it was the most beautiful gift in the world – which it always was.

Chapter Twenty-Eight

'I don't envy you in the least, angels/and I can wade grief./But if by the side of the path one/particular bush rises/the rowanberry . . .'

This particular lyric intrigued Elena as she committed it to memory; not so much for what it said as because of the precise date the poetess had noted. It was written on the day Michael had seen his sister's apparition in black on one of the canal bridges. She told Marion about her fleeting appearance in the city, that Ascension Day, and Marion said, Yes, it was natural, all her emotions had been bent on home as she wrote that poem, and when she thought of home she thought of the little bridges.

A joyful letter arrived from Michael. He said he had never ceased having an 'inward conversation' with her, his sister, and he would come as soon as he possibly could to be with her. Unhappily there was a severe outbreak of scarlet fever in the area; in the absence of a genuine doctor he was doing his best; it might be several weeks before he could have a break. She would be glad to know that her nephew was happy and well; the widow with whom he was lodging was a warm-hearted, motherly person, who had taken the boy to her heart.

Scarlet fever was also rife in the city, besides other infections. People weakened already by hunger were dying like flies; but the hosts of the dead were more than replaced by refugees of one kind and another. They slept in passageways, along the embankment, on station platforms. The famine grew worse; the situation was out of hand. It was at this time that a purge of the highest-ranking officials in charge of supplies took place, and Elena's former husband found himself promoted and entitled to a fine separate house. He had very soon got rid of his mistress, and was living with his still half-crazed wife. The little girl, too, was back with them. Elena picked this up from one of her neighbours, a housemaid who knew everyone's business.

One evening when Elena came home tired and depressed she found her friend in a distraught state. The croupier who had lived upstairs had died, and today had been his funeral. Marion, who had only glimpsed him once in passing, had nevertheless become very upset when she heard the coffin being bumped down the stairs. She was pacing the room, as Elena came in; her fingers, holding a cigarette, shook. 'Just imagine, Elena, now he *knows*! The only thing that matters! Now he *knows* and we don't! Or perhaps' (she shuddered) 'he *doesn't* know! Isn't it awful? How can we bear to go on living?'

Elena sometimes asked the same question.

She had gone back on the streets. There was no money left, no jobs to be had, even in service; she had tried everywhere. At least, she would still be mistress of her soul. Marion was horrified at the idea, and guilty at being in the position of having to live off her friend's degradation; but in the end there seemed to be no alternative. In a city where nearly everyone whored in the spirit, selling each other, it was almost a virtue merely to sell your own body. So Elena dolled herself up, as much as her poverty allowed, plastering her face with cheap lipstick, powder and mascara, took her courage in both hands, and sallied forth. She found the street much changed: the shop fronts dingier, the passers-by more derelict, drunken and uncouth, the whores dirtier, shabbier, more sullen and desperate. Half-frozen in the cold November fog, they hugged their poor dreams like the little dying match seller in the fable.

There was little enough money in it. Though Elena charged as little as before, despite the huge rise in living costs, she found she was overcharging. At the mention of her price, men laughed, or swore at her, and walked away to one of the other girls. While the flesh of animals was astronomically dear, beyond the purse of any but the rich, the price of human flesh had never been cheaper. It was perhaps the only commodity in the city whose supply was even greater than the ravenous demand. The police had long ago stopped taking the prostitutes into custody; with so many thousands of them on the streets, it was one way of pretending that the employment situation was under control. The main danger (apart from disease) was of attacks by the customers themselves. The ill-lit streets were an open chequebook to the sadist and the murderer. In one week alone, in November, twelve whores were murdered. The authorities, while using all their means, etc., were rather relieved than otherwise.

To minimize the risk, Elena operated mostly before night fell. If business was really bad and she had to stay out after dark, she teamed up with another girl – the girl, in fact, with whom she had 'changed rooms'. They bumped into each other on Elena's third day out, and agreed, over a glass of cheap gin, to sink their past in a common necessity. Now they were no longer mistress and servant, wife and mistress, they became quite good chums.

Most of Elena's customers were factory workers, dock-workers, off-duty soldiers and sailors – working men, short-timers who could afford only a few coins for a few minutes. Down a lane from the street where she solicited stood the ancient cathedral, now disused, and usually she took her clients there. The portals gave shelter and a little privacy, but she was close enough to the public street to scream, if necessary, and bring help – not from the public or the police, need-less to say, but from other whores. They stuck together in a kind of trade union. Usually help was even closer to hand, in the neighbour-ing portals; another girl with her customer, or squatting against the wall, relieving herself.

With the rare 'gentleman' who came by, Elena found that to earn a decent sum she was expected to submit to other unpleasant things besides, or instead of, intercourse. They sometimes asked if they could piss, or even shit, on her; or if she would do it to them. One customer asked if he could stuff silver coins up her cunt: she could keep as many as she was prepared to admit. Some only wanted to bugger her. Another gentleman (whom she thought she recognized from one of her ex-husband's business dinners) took Elena and her friend to a cemetery. He fucked her friend against a tombstone, and then made Elena lie on the grassy grave mound. After he had come, she felt something on her thigh above her stocking; when she looked it was a fat, black slug. Shuddering, she shook it off with her petticoat.

She would take a man back to her room only if she was fairly sure he was gentlemanly and quiet. Then she would cough loudly and chat outside the door, fumbling for her key, to warn Marion to hide herself behind the blanket. They would joke about these visits after-wards, over a meal or a cigarette – to treat it as a joke was the only way of dealing with it; laughter in the trenches, so to speak. They would go into a mock Southern belle conversation: 'A sho' hope ma' gen'lem'n caller did not discommode yo', honey?' 'Land sakes, no indeed, 'Lena! He sho' is a most sensitive and refahned character!' 'Ah'm so glad yo' think so! Ah will admit to yo', ah'm most im-pressed bah him, honey! He's bin a genuwine ayengel to little ol' me!' – a reference, which made them both chuckle, to the poetess's verse claiming that angels rent the other half of any room where we happen to be living.

Chapter Twenty-Nine

There was sporadic terrorism. Two highly placed officials were blown up in their car. Demands for democracy were painted over the authorities' democratic slogans. Desperate to hold the shaky fabric together, the authorities were yielding to minor concessions, so making their final collapse inevitable. In the initial stages of the liberalizing strategy, Marion had been allowed to return to the city. Now, in the onset of winter, she was told at the police station that she need report no more than once a month; better news still, her request for a pass to visit her brother in their home town was granted.

Elena worked hard to save her rail fare; even overstepping her firm bounds of what sexual behaviour to tolerate. As if sensing some new and greater disaster round the corner, her customers' taste for sensation and perversity was growing ever more acute. A dark spider, couched somewhere in the city, spun very swiftly and smoothly a whole network of vice and pleasure. Elena worked now in the house adjoining the Arts Theatre, which itself became an artistic cabaret, with fine food, fine wine, fine girls. The brothel and the cabaret worked hand in glove. Elena paid commission to the madam for the use of one of the rooms during the day. Compared with the icy streets, it was luxury, and there was a better class of customer. Men came for the food and the dance, and to ogle the pretty girls. It was natural to end a good evening in the tasteful debauchery of the house next door.

It was also safer. The murderer, who mutilated 'professional' women in some unspeakable way was still active. Some said there was a whole gang of them – anti-women and anti-Semitic too, to judge by the slogans they chalked on the walls above their bleeding victims. It was safe to sit in the cabaret, drinking and chatting, and then lead the gentleman quickly into the brothel where there were friendly faces all round. You could take more chances with what you let them get up to, and earn more money. One evening she allowed herself to be laced so tightly into a corset that the man could get his large hands right round her waist. She all but passed out. That was not enough for him; he had to bind her with ropes, tied round the chair and cutting painfully into her breasts. She drew the line at being gagged, but let him lash parts of her body with a cane, after which she masturbated him and finally let him drench her with his urine. There was a large sum for this abuse, enough to buy Marion's rail ticket and have some over for the rent.

When he had gone, she felt sore and sick; but there was another gentleman diner from the cabaret whom she had promised to entertain. He was waiting in the lounge, listening to the gramophone and flicking through the pornographic magazines. She was tempted to fly down the stairs, but she always tried to keep a promise. Fortunately he was a real gentleman, and sexually impotent, as it happened. He only really needed to look at her body and have a pleasant conversation. She was soon out of the brothel and walking home along a complicated well-lit route.

The fog was thick, though, and there were few people on the streets. She could hear footsteps behind and she walked faster, frightened. The footsteps started running, and she started to run too. But she was seized from behind, a snarl told her to keep quiet or she'd be done for, and she was being pulled into an alleyway.

She remembers hoping he was only a thief, yet sure in her heart he was the murderer. His hands started squeezing her throat, she was choking, looking straight into his face. Though it was black in the unlit alley she saw enough of him to register that she knew this man – it was the sadist who had left her bleeding on the floor of her room and who had raped and tortured her in the prison cell. He had a beard now, but there was no mistaking those eyes. He released his hands and she was lying on the ground, gulping breath. He was pushing up her skirt, tugging at her thin panties; she was so exhausted she could do nothing, except pray he was only a rapist. She remembers looking at him in a dazed way, and even recalls helping him, lifting her foot so that he could tug the panties over her high-heeled shoe. It was better to get it over with; either he would rape her and be done, or he would produce the knife and complete what he had twice tried to do; anyway, the sooner the better.

But as he knelt down between her thighs, she vaguely heard the sound of a car drawing up at the end of the alley. A motor horn blared. The man jumped up and ran off into the alley. Elena, too shocked to cry or speak, found herself being helped to her feet by an old lady in a fur coat. Was she all right? Elena nodded, feeling her throat, and the old lady stooped to pick up the knickers; Elena stuffed them in her coat pocket. 'We'd better not stay around here,' said the old lady, and helped her to the car. She said she was on her way home from a concert. It was lucky she had glanced aside into the alleyway as she drove by and caught sight of something. She had been tempted to go on, not become involved – but that was to opt out of humanity. She had pulled up, reversed, and come back. She had spent all her life in this city, and never could she remember such terrible crimes.

She asked Elena where she lived, as they drove along, and said it was not far out of her way. Elena fumbled for a cigarette, and started to cry. The kindly old lady said that was the best thing to do, that would make her feel better. Elena dried her eyes and, relaxing a little, looked at her saviour. She had a mop of grey hair, and expensive-looking earrings; she caught a glimpse of a pearl necklace inside her fur coat. It was not surprising: only a very wealthy woman could have afforded a car. Then she glanced at the driving wheel and started to tremble. She tried to stop herself from trembling so violently, and to answer yes and no to the old lady's conversation as if nothing was wrong. The old lady's hands on the wheel were unusually large and rough; she thought she saw hair on them. She looked down at the floor of the car, but the old lady's legs and feet were hidden by a long gown.

She listened to the old lady's deep, melodious voice, and knew it belonged to her gentle, impotent customer. The old lady turned off into a deserted brickyard, saying that she really must excuse her manners but she was dying for a pee, couldn't wait, it was the shock of what had happened. She stopped the engine and picked up her large handbag from the floor, turning with a pleasant grin towards her passenger. 'Have one of my cigarettes,' she said, opening her bag and taking out a small axe. Simultaneously Elena drove her stiffened fingers at the old lady's eyes. The old lady cried out, dropped the axe, clawed at her eyes. Elena leapt out of the car and ran for her life.

Elena was more or less herself again after a couple of quiet days. They discussed whether she should report it, but decided it would be a waste of time. The police despised whores and hated Jews, so there was no reason to think they would want the sadist behind bars. He knew her address, which was disturbing, but there was nothing to be done except put the chain on the door which her first husband had promised and forgotten. The poetess did not like to leave her friend alone, but Elena insisted. She was not one to brood on things. So a week before Christmas, Marion took the train to see her brother, the happy and sad meeting of which she has written. ('Diamond nights above the ancient town . . . cautiously I tread on crystals.')

Chapter Thirty

When Elena told the girls about her narrow escape, and to spread the word not to trust kindly old ladies in fur coats, they were very concerned for her. It brought her to the notice of the master of ceremonies at the cabaret – an avowed homosexual – who asked her if she could dance. Elena had enjoyed dancing when she was very young, without being especially talented, and answered truthfully, Yes, she liked dancing, but wasn't very good. The homosexual looked at her legs appreciatively, and offered her a place in the chorus line. One of his girls had gone down with scarlet fever. The money would not be great, but it would be regular. Elena jumped at the offer.

She practised for a week and then was thrown into the deep end. She soon came to enjoy the spirited dances, of which the cancan was the *pièce de résistance*. The girls were good fun to be with; and she felt better for the exercise, regular hours, and the meal she could have each day at the club. She had grown skinny but now her clothes fitted her again; she had a sparkle in her eye and was glad to wake up each morning. It was harmless fun, watching the eyes of the diners stand out of their heads as the girls kicked their legs in the air; the wild cancan even made *her* feel sexy; she liked the moment when each girl in turn, at the finale, did a reckless 'splits', a series of *cracks*, like automatic gunfire, as their thighs smacked the wood floor – or like parachute jumping, 'Go! Go! Go!' She liked the sight of fat, rosy faces flying up, the fat, white, wildly clapping hands. It was good that it could end there; that she could go to her dressing room, take a shower, maybe have a cool glass of champagne and go home.

One afternoon, after a matinée performance, she was pulling off her black stockings when there was a knock on the dressing-room door. Another girl opened it, and Elena was astonished, and delighted, to see Peter standing there. He sported a beard and looked, naturally, a little older, but it was the same Peter, bubbling with good humour. She popped open a bottle of champagne, and they chatted merrily while she finished changing. All was well with him, and with some of their other friends — not all. She listened sadly as he mentioned the names of those who had *sunk*, in one way or other. He had gone to earth, in one of the poorest areas. He had mounted one small exhibition in a local wine shop, but it had aroused hostility and been closed by the police and the paintings confiscated. That was warning enough. He was painting, but not showing. Now, things looked a shade more hopeful. Somebody had seen Elena in the chorus line and passed on the news. He had sold a dud painting – highly acceptable! a horse! (they both laughed), and decided to blow it all at the cabaret. Now, she must come and meet his wife. Yes, he had got married, to a salesgirl at the wine shop (his eyes sparkled!), and they had a young baby already – a trifle early!

Right now was as good a time as any, between performances. She walked with him along the river, past the docks, to a part of the embankment where grimy, cheap cafés served the docks and the nearby factories. Snow drifted in the iron day and fell on deserted tables overlooking the river. Peter led her through the café, past two or three morose drinkers, up rickety stairs and down a windowless corridor. He knocked at a door and threw it open; spoke a cheerful hello, saying he'd brought an old friend. Elena found herself in a garret room not much larger than a cupboard. At first she could hardly see: the tiny window admitted hardly any of what little light there was. Peter's buxom young wife was sitting, a baby on her lap, changing its nappy. The stench of shit and sweat and stale cooking smells was awful. Elena tried to breathe through her mouth.

The harassed mother, hair over her eyes, cradled her baby in one arm and stretched out the other. She had heard a lot about Elena, she said. She smiled crookedly. She was plump and ordinary, a healthy animal. (And she would have to be, thought Elena, in this hole.) Peter squatted down under the sink, and waved Elena to take the only other chair. It did not feel very safe, and she sat well forward, gingerly, playing with the smiling infant. There was good humour in the foul air, and she could see they were happy. The mother scooped the dirty nappy into a ball, gave the baby's bottom a last wipe, and dropped the ball into a pail of water.

'There's another room,' said Peter, leaping to his feet. He led her out into the passage again and opened another door. This room was even tinier and darker. He lit an oil lamp. There was an easel, and some canvases resting against the damp walls. 'See what I've been doing,' he invited.

He held one of the canvases close to the lamp, and Elena gasped. Even in the smoky, yellow light the colours jumped at her. She had to blink. 'Do you recognize it?' he asked eagerly. She saw that it was the garden of her house, with the line of trees, and the tall grass; and it was without question the picture he had painted when Michael had been recovering from TB. But he had transformed it. The red of her skirt in the trees had gone, had been turned into hundreds of bright poppy heads splashed indiscriminately among the green; and she had reappeared as a lady in blue, in the immediate foreground, carrying a blue parasol, and with a little boy following her closely. But what had changed most of all was the colour, the light: it blazed, shimmered, ran, without shadows; so that the painting seemed on the verge of disappearing, it was so clearly one particular moment on a particular spring day, a moment that had never happened. 'I like it,' she said quietly; and he grinned with pleasure just as he started to have doubts himself. 'Do you recognize this one?' he said; and he showed her the painting he had made while they picnicked in the woods: the two naked girls sitting with the two fully clothed men. She told him to take it away – she was ashamed how fat she had been. But as he took it from her she held on to it and looked at it more carefully. He had changed it too; not so much, but with striking effect. She, with her fleshy sides and breasts, was now much more shockingly, indecently nude, set against the starchier but rakish-looking men. And the guitarist's girlfriend was now sitting, dressed and demure, in the background, as if she had opted out. It made one wonder just what was going on – as if, right after the poses broke, the three main figures threw themselves into shameless fucking. Indeed, the fuck was already there, in the picture. And the same shadowless brightness, new to his work, as in the other picture. She told him so.

Then he showed her, proudly, an entirely new picture that had grown out of his experiments with the others. It was a painting of his young, plump wife, suckling their child. She saw that the very ordinary cocotte whom he had married was really very pretty, her face suffused with love. And she was so like a luscious, pickable, rosy apple – the sort you used to be able to buy from a stall, when she had first come to the city. You could not buy them any longer. But Peter's wife reminded her of those apples so sharply that saliva flooded her mouth.

Chapter Thirty-One

As winter gave occasional glimpses of spring, Marion came back. She was happy to have been with her brother, yet happy to return to her city and to see Elena again. And there was a chance, a whisper, that Michael might be allowed to return soon, for an extended period if not for good. He was frantically busy, but miraculously had avoided contagion so far; and her nephew was well, too – and here was a drawing he had made, for Elena, to thank her for her lovely gift. They chuckled over the drawing of Auntie Elena and the boy making faces at the monkey in the zoo. But the poetess sighed, and fell into a gloomy silence, and spoke again about sin, betrayal, the impossibility of redemption. Elena saw signs of the same obscure guilt in the next poem she was asked to memorize, the one that says 'how deeply faithless we are, which is/to say: how true we are to ourselves.'

Elena was ill. This in itself was unusual, as she had always kept remarkably healthy, in spite of everything, but the illness was also strange and hard to pin down. It started as a dry irritating cough. She thought it was simply a cold, and cut down her smoking. It persisted, and added to it was a more or less continuous ache in her left temple. She was alarmed to think she might be developing scarlet fever, which was proving unusually persistent and virulent. Her vision began to be disturbed, and she felt also a peculiar icy grip at the back of her neck, so that she could not bend her head foward. Sometimes there were remissions of one or other of these symptoms, and she thought she might be getting better; but always they returned. Then, for some hours during the day, she would fall into a sleepy, almost a trance, state. When she woke up, she would complain to Marion of the profound darkness in her head, of being unable to think, unable to find words. She started to have trouble with her speech; instead of articulate sentences she spoke disjointedly. Sometimes she would say, over and over, the word 'pain'.

She became prone to hallucinations and recurrent nightmares. She saw herself treading on piles of human heads, alive, half-buried in mud; she was convinced that leeches were sucking her breasts; she dreamt, night after night, of a huge water rat sliding up a sandy beach towards her.

She had to give up her job at the cabaret. She went to a doctor, but he could find nothing the matter. He advised plenty of rest. She was getting plenty of that already; in fact it was her sleepiness that alarmed Marion more than anything, since normally they shared a tendency to insomnia. In her secret thoughts, Marion was afraid of a brain tumour. If she could only see a specialist; but none was available even if they could have afforded the fee. She could only watch Elena, write to Michael for his advice, and worry.

The water rat stopped appearing in her dreams. Maybe it had gone to see a rat psychologist, Marion joked. But soon another nightmare took its place. A man, stoutly built and with swarthy features, entered her room while she slept; lay on her, and tried to murder her. Worse still, she began to hallucinate this murderous vision by day.

Elena was quite bright enough to know that several, perhaps all, of these visions might be explained by events in the past: the city's derelict sleepers she had stepped over; the rat in the prison that had crashed against its bars close to her head; her recent terrifying experience. Yet she had resolutely put these behind her. She had felt happier than for a long time; why should such horrors suddenly start up in front of her? Anyway, the man who was murdering her was not the rapist, nor the wolf in sheep's clothing.

The poet – doctor – old-age pensioner (as he signed himself) could only express his concern, and suggest she keep a record of her dreams. The illness seemed to be getting worse. Elena was sure she was going mad.

At her wit's end, Marion climbed the stairs to the room of the new janitor. He was a distinguished-looking man, grey at the temples, who kept himself very much to himself; rumour had it that he was a medical man who had retired early because of ill health. Marion hoped that he might be able to suggest something, followed one of her hunches. She was in luck. He was extremely courteous, inviting her into his pleasant book-lined room, and offering her coffee. He knew of her – enjoyed some of her work – was delighted to meet her. What could he do for her? She asked him if he knew anything about the mind. He smiled and said no. No one did! But as a matter of fact he had been a specialist in schizophrenic disorders, at such-and-such mental hospital (mentioning the notorious place in which Michael had been briefly incarcerated). His breakdown and premature retirement were the result of being compelled to carry out inhuman, unjustifiable treatment. Marion looked guiltily over her shoulder. The man's gaze was firm. It was a sign of changing times that he dared to voice such things. She warmed to him and told him about her friend. They arranged that Elena should come up to see him the very next day.

Elena went every day to the janitor to spend a couple of hours in talk, mostly about her past and her dreams (he too asked her to keep note of her dreams). She could not see any signs of improvement after their talks, but he was a very pleasant, attractive man and she enjoyed the visits. They were the happiest part of the day. She strove to please him by dreaming some interesting dreams. One that she did not relate to him was a dream in which the janitor undressed her to give her a thorough examination and then made love to her. She recalled him saying, 'This is poetry not science', as he sucked her nipple.

He tried hypnotizing her, but she was not easily 'put under', and even when she was, he found her not very forthcoming. It proved more fruitful to invite her, in full consciousness, to talk about her dreams and nightmares, and what she associated them with. He was sure the answer to her illness lay far back in her childhood, which she insisted had been a happy one. He unveiled to her the mysteries of the Electra complex, and of the profound battle between the super-ego and the id. She was impressed to think that her humble mind, which found difficulty with even the simplest crossword, could contain such engrossing conflicts. (She imagined a fortress on a hill, its battlements lined with helmeted warriors, and an alien army constantly driving forward and constantly being repulsed.) She was quite proud of herself. But it did not seem to her to have very much to do with her illness.

The retired psychologist was very anxious to discover if she remembered, as a child, having seen her parents making love. Elena convinced herself, after a time, that she had. She had slept in their room, and thought she could dimly recall their bedclothes heaving, just like the mountainous waves that piled against the cliffs in winter. The psychologist was very pleased. Almost certainly, Elena had thought her father was killing her mother; she *wanted* him to, because of the Electra complex, which had naturally resulted in a feeling of guilt and a need to repress the memory. Now the memory had emerged. The man in the nightmare was not murdering her, he was making love to her, and he was her father.

Elena, out shopping, caught sight of her pale, tragic, urchin face reflected in a shop window, and marvelled at the incest and murder seething under the chic fur hat Marion had bought her.

Had her father ever got into bed with her? Yes, once or twice, to comfort her when they were alone in the house and there was thunder and lightning. And had he made any sexual advances? No, of course he had not. But perhaps she had felt his erection without realizing what it was? The psychologist looked so anxious for this to be so, that Elena said, Perhaps, she thought she might have done. The psychologist nodded, pleased. Elena's dry cough could be explained by a childhood desire to fellate her father. Beyond that he could not penetrate.

Elena was sure this was not the case. The man lying with his hands around her throat was not her beloved father; and whoever it was, he was not making love to her but murdering her. However, she kept these thoughts to herself and pretended to agree with him. She liked him very much; he was very intelligent – even if a bit stupid in her case – and gentle. She loved his deep grey eyes and grey temples.

She was still very sick, but could no longer afford to pay him even the tiny sums which he said were essential if the treatment was to work, so she had to stop going to see him.

Then, as the snows melted and the lilac broke into leaf, her illness cleared up, almost overnight. She closed her memory to it, and did not even recognize the slouching beast and pile of human heads when they turned up in one of Michael's poems later on.

Chapter Thirty-Two

The poet had been allowed back, for an unspecified period. It was summer; he came alone; his nephew was working for exams at school and it did not seem worth taking him away from his kindly foster mother just at this time. He could join them in the holidays if Michael was still here.

Elena had started work again at the cabaret. In honour of a triple event, Michael's homecoming, Ascension Day and Liberation Day — which seemed worth celebrating this year — she persuaded her boss to throw a backstage party. She asked Peter and his wife, and a few other friends — but not the psychologist, who she thought would be too serious minded for such goings-on. There was a full and generous house that evening, everyone in holiday mood; her friends watching, enjoying themselves, and joining Elena and the girls afterwards, with much laughter and champagne and embracing. There was nothing like the cancan, with good food and plenty of drink to start a party off well — especially when most of the girls, some still in their costumes or brazenly getting changed, were among the guests! Peter did his best to look sad when explaining that his wife was having to baby sit, but his eyes sparkled. The many mirrors created even more gorgeous plump-thighed, bosomy women, he hardly knew where to look next; and Michael too was feeling thoroughly in the mood, happy to be back in the city he loved and glad to have handed over the task of healing the sick to a real doctor, one who was 'back from the grave'.

And the gay impresario, with his red cravat and flowing brown hair, was in his element too, gliding around, putting his arm round men and women alike, keeping their glasses charged.

The director of *Snow Queen*, who had also recently returned after a long and mysterious absence, came in, late; exclaimed 'My dear Michael!' and rushed towards him. They bear-hugged, and toasted freedom and the future. There was laughter, and a few tears. Almost everyone had a peculiar feeling that after many false dawns here at last was the true one.

Glasses were getting smashed at a good rate and the party was a raging success. Elena was pleased at her idea. She was none too sober herself, she had to lean on people's shoulders rather a lot. Everyone was listing, but nobody had become violent, just bursting with jollity and affection. They danced, or rather lurched around in each other's arms, kissing whoever happened to meet one's lips. When the party looked like falling asleep, some of the girls livened it up by putting on the cancan music and doing it impromptu, in their ordinary clothes, hoisting their skirts up, which somehow made it even more erotic and enjoyable and risqué. Peter was perhaps drunker than anybody, and he put his hand up one of the dancers' skirts when she had flopped down on a seat to recover, but nobody minded. It was good to let one's hair down and do the things one always longed to do but dared not. The gay impresario challenged Peter when he bragged that he always painted with his prick, and Peter said he would show them right there and then if Elena would strip off to him. 'Go on then!' the dancing girls giggled; and Elena took off her clothes and Peter unzipped his trousers and pulled out his penis, to claps and squeals, and someone gave him a large paper towel, and he dipped his penis in a glass of red wine and proceeded to draw a quite respectable nude. The drawing was passed from hand to hand and much admired.

Everyone said how good it was to be such good, loving people together, and that sex was a beautiful thing; and the drama director invited Elena to lie down on the floor and close her eyes and just enjoy everybody stroking her, very gently, not in lust but in love. After a little persuasion she did (she was actually very glad to lie down and close her eyes), and people of all sexes kneeled beside her and started stroking and kissing all the parts of her body. They asked her if she was enjoying it and she said, yes, it was lovely, and they should go on. Finally everybody had got bored with it except the director and one of the girls' husbands (Peter was flat out in a chair unconscious). Elena, her thighs wide apart, could feel fingers moving gently in her. Sleepily she asked which one of them was doing it or if it was both of them, and they said, yes, it was both of them. She murmured that it made her feel very pampered.

Then there were other incidents of which Michael and Elena and Marion, and probably many other guests, felt ashamed later on. After they had snatched an hour's sleep, on the floor or in armchairs, the three of them walked a fuddled Peter along the river bank to his home and family. They were silent and embarrassed.

The fresh breeze cleared their heads. It was not yet the middle of the night, yet the dawn was already here, a pearly sky, the low sun flashing on the river (the sun hardly set at all this time of the year, the time of the white nights). There was freedom in the air at last. An excited ripple had gone around the diners last night: the cashier had been listening to a transistor radio and news had come through of elections to be held. Nobody had been able to confirm the rumour, and she was rather a scatterbrained creature, but they could feel that the future, an infinitely better future, was being borne slowly down the river towards them. Michael was happy as he felt the wind and the soft midnight on his face, and it stirred an image. 'We must blow away the corruption,' he said. They all felt that what had happened that night had belonged to the old corrupt world and it would not and must not happen again.

They climbed the steps – a little sluggishly! – to the famous bronze statue. From here they would take in the whole silent and serene city: this mother of cities, with its forty times forty churches and seven hills. The great white cathedral dome sparkled in the centre; wide boulevards and prospects radiated from it, and number-less narrow ways with numerous stone bridges over the shining canals, all silent now, waiting. And dominating it all, the winding, blue, eternally feminine river.

Even the factories and slums smudged into the beauty of their capital, this morning; and there were still green spots, quiet secluded parks and gardens, with gushing fountains. The city had changed its name yet again, but that made no difference. It astonished them to see how beautiful it still was, in spite of everything, and their hearts overflowed with thanksgiving.

They rested at the sleeping café for a few minutes, before setting off home. Peter, sober now, poured them some refreshing lemonade. The house slept. They took their glasses out to the embankment tables, and talked in whispers. Peter said he felt ashamed of his vulgar act, and wanted to paint Elena properly. She protested that he had a beautiful model in his wife, but he said he had exhausted her as a model, though not as a wife; he needed a new model, or a new old one. She smiled; he would never change or grow up!

He painted her at a quiet bathing place, and caught the mid-summer sun pouring on to her wet body; caught her plump young breasts and broad thighs (for she needed to lose a few pounds again) at perhaps their moment of perfection – though it is rash to say so with Elena; caught her warm eyes, narrowed slightly against the sunlight, the snub nose and rosy lips, her round cheeks blushing and, like her nipples, bringing an extra colour and richness to the ripe peach; caught the wet flowing hair (for she wore it long now). She blushed scarlet when she looked at his painting and put her hand to her chin to see if it was really so plump; and he slapped his hand teasingly on her belly and moved it down and rasped it against her bush of hair, and told her she was gorgeous, and to get dressed and come home and have a glass of wine.

Chapter Thirty-Three

She brooded on the events of the party. Every so often, she felt unhappy in relation to her soul – corrupt – like a rich man's constant awareness of being over-full. When she felt like this she tried to get away on her own. In the old days, she had gone up into the mountain to stay with the nuns in their convent. Walking in the clear mountain air, praying in the chapel, watching the smiling, toothless old nuns drawing water from the spring to wash their clothes, had restored her and she felt light again. Once, she had spent a whole summer sharing their life and their habit. Now, there were no religious orders left, but she seized the chance of going for a month to the university, as a voluntary guest in their common cold experimental unit. Most of the time she was left completely on her own, in her small bare room. She could think and pray, and grow light again. When it was over and she returned home – with a heavy cold – she felt like a young girl waiting for her first communion.

The cashier had mis-heard about the elections, but you could no more stop the feeling that great things were on the way than you could stop the wind from blowing and scattering the leaves. You could feel it in Elena's house. People whistled a few bars of a popular freedom song as they passed on the stairs. Everybody was using the front entrance again. Most of the rich had hurriedly left their apartments, abandoning furniture, carpets, and labour-saving devices. Their servants were living like lords, selling off bits and pieces and getting drunk on the proceeds. The few rich people who stayed on, quaking in their shoes, dressed in their oldest clothes, and paid their servants to live with them as equals.

There was talk of turning the apartments back into single rooms, and assigning them again to artists; the janitor said the architect had already been to work out what alterations would be needed. There was little bread, perhaps even less than before, but a lot of eager discussion, in rooms all over the city, about art and philosophy. Artists crawled one by one out of their graves, though many would not rise till the Day of Judgment. The gay impresario was actually a choreographer of genius, and he quickly turned his cancan girls into a competent ballet troupe; the theatre once more echoed to good music and ringing words. Pigtailed schoolgirls turned overnight into actresses and prima ballerinas.

The chauffeur, Elena's neighbour, having decamped with his master and mistress, Michael had his old room again; but not for long. Elena found a more urgent use for it, and the poet was soon back sharing with the girls. One morning the newspaper showed surly pictures of a dozen high officials, arrested for misappropriation of public funds. They were to stand trial for their crimes in a court of justice (this in itself was sensational). One of the criminal faces belonged to Elena's second husband. She could not bring herself to feel very sorry for him; but she worried about his poor little stepdaughter. What would happen to her? Would they punish the criminal's family too, as so often happened? She made some inquiries, and eventually called at a sumptuous house, in the best suburb. She hardly recognized her former imperious mistress in the dull-witted and shocked creature who answered her ring. The servants had knifed their dog, threatened to mutilate her and her daughter, and stripped the house clean. Elena found the girl sitting on the floor, vacant, stinking.

Elena and Michael wangled it with the janitor to have the woman and her daughter moved into the room next to Elena's, where they would at least be unnoticed and have someone to keep a friendly eye on them. The woman seemed sane enough, merely stupefied.

Elena was out of work now, since she scarcely had the figure to be a ballet dancer; but Peter was selling some of his paintings and she earned a bit by sitting for him. The rent had been cut; there was very little else to spend money on.

The room was cramped, but they could sit in the garden or take walks. Anyway, they got on marvellously together. Now and again Marion would virtually throw Elena out of the room when she wanted to discuss her work in private with Michael. 'Go and buy some cigarettes,' she would command. But she could laugh at her weaknesses – that imperious streak, and her jealousy over the warm-hearted widow who wrote to Michael every other day. She – Marion – radiated high spirits and energy; Elena wondered why she had ever considered her shy and withdrawn. Only when she was writing – then she seemed to lock herself away within herself. She wrote with her stern lips pressed together, whereas her brother quietly spoke his verses to himself as he paced the floor.

In general they seemed to live as one, anticipating each other's thoughts. Michael even claimed to believe that his sister had saved his life when he lay dying with consumption: for at the same time she had been suffering from Graves's disease, and Graves's disease, he said, acted as a cure for consumption. This was not particularly fair to Elena, who had nursed him day and night; but she smiled at the odd idea, good-humouredly. There were a lot of jokes and laughs, and running about like children. They indulged in childish word games, and competed with each other as to which could see the furthest – they were proud of their keen sight, which they ascribed to the fact that their father had been an eye surgeon! Marion possessed a consuming interest in, and compassion for, the dead, and she made Michael talk freely at last about their brother. He was a poet too, they said: better than either of them. Elena, surprised, asked where she could find his work. 'Here,' they said, and they both tapped their foreheads. Elena said she'd like to share it too – wouldn't it be safer? They said, yes it would, but she already had enough poems to carry. Nonsense, said Elena; one thing she did have was a good memory. So they told her their brother's poems and she remembered them, though they seemed to her even more difficult to understand than Michael's.

So they lived together, childishly and soberly, seriously and play-fully. They were excited by the freedom in the air, but the brother and sister were even more excited by the inner freedom given them by their gift.

In his poem to his sister, written at this time and passed to Elena to be learnt, Michael made the feminine observation that the sunburnt arm he kissed had a strip of white left by her bracelet (for he had given her a bracelet too, long ago); and in her poem to him, Marion made the masculine generalization that the whole earth had been passed down to him and he had shared it with everyone.

It appeared that the 'pre-Gutenberg age', as Marion ironically called it, was coming to an end. Michael's editor called – he had been reinstated in his post – and clearly bore no grudge against the poet for getting him into trouble. He was bubbling with eagerness to bring out a new book . . . and a book of his sister's too. Slim volumes of new verse that could be rushed out; then they could work more slowly on collected editions; he had an idea that the previous aborted edition was probably still in type, somewhere. They were given quite a lordly advance on the new slim volumes, and with amazing speed the books were rushed out. Equally amazingly, the limited editions were gobbled up on the bookstands within minutes.

After that, there were enormously popular readings in the crowded, intimate atmosphere of the Arts Theatre. Elena went to hear them a couple of times, with her psychologist friend; but as she knew all their work by heart anyway she got rather bored, the second time. But she enjoyed the build-up of tension as the audience waited for the poets. And especially the superbly theatrical entrance of Marion, sweeping a way through the crowd, in her long white dress and black cloak! She deserved her triumph, after so many disasters, and who could blame her if she enjoyed it? The fact was, that although Elena had at first not thought so, she was strikingly attractive. There was this slim, elegant figure, the pale, classically chiselled features, the big, lustrous eyes. Her one imperfection ('and yet your body had a flaw'), a slight 'break' in the line of her nose, gave to her face a stern Roman character, made her more beautiful. She had had her hair cut in a new style for the readings: short, and with a fringe that was handsomely boyish. And the way she bowed her slim, swan-like neck to take the applause! But Michael tilted his slightly over-large and comical head back, his gaze birdlike.

Such was the city, at this time – black satin cloaks and black bread. But at least the bread appeared to be shared out more equally, which made it taste better.

Workers demonstrated, and struck for their rights. The newspapers ceased publication, the radio went off the air. There were rumbles of violence, hints of war. The enemies of the people would not give up their privileges without a bitter fight. Rumours flew that they had formed an army, and were marching to attack the city. Decidedly there were terrorists at work from within. One day a parcel bomb exploded at the post office, killing or maiming the sorters. Then, more dreadful, there was the train supposed to be bringing an important, and friendly man; but as it drew very slowly into the station, it blew up — packed with high explosives that killed hundreds assembled on the platform, including several dignitaries.

Chapter Thirty-Four

The defences were holding, beyond the river to the south. Every available man had been thrown into the desperate struggle to defend freedom, or the possibility of freedom. (Peter was out there somewhere, sitting in a mud-filled trench, his rifle in one hand and his sketch pad in the other.) Shells smashed into the suburbs, but the heart of the city was still intact; above all, the white dome of the cathedral still stood, sublime, indifferent to the shell bursts. And now, in the face of death, it gave covering and solace to thousands of bare-headed worshippers — old women, children, soldiers withdrawn from the front line to rest, and their sweethearts; prostitutes, who no longer needed to hoist their skirts under the shelter of its granite, but had useful, honourable work to do in the arms factories.

When the war was still only distant gunfire that might have been thunder, the word spread that fighting had broken out in the town where Michael's nephew was living. Marion had turned white on hearing this, and said she must go there at once. Her fingers were all thumbs, and Elena helped her to pack her suitcase.

She had fought her way on to the last train leaving the city. Nothing more had been heard of her, but that was only to be expected in the chaos. Her brother trusted his intuition, which told him that she, and his nephew too, were safe. Their 'inward conversation' continued. In contrast he found it hard to recall the features of the plump widow. He still thought of her as that, even though — in the perfunctory manner of the time – she had become his wife. It came to him in a dream that she was dead.

The large apartments – once the reception rooms for dukes and ambassadors – had been turned into an emergency hospital. Mattresses overflowed into the corridors; the place seethed with an air of crisis and *ad hoc* surgery as though it were a field hospital. Effectively it was. They could hear the shells exploding close by and many civilians were brought in.

Both Elena and Michael were serving here: she in a Red Cross uniform and he with a surgeon's coat over his khaki. They saw little of each other. Michael worked the day shift and she the night. Both, in reality, worked day and night, since there were so few doctors and nurses to cope with the ever-increasing casualties; but even when they were in the wards together there was no chance for anything but a smile in passing. Sometimes not even that. What he glimpsed of her work deepened his respect for her.

Though she had never seen, or even imagined, such horrors, she felt strong, serene even, because for the first time ever she was doing important and necessary work. And the enemy could be identified and fought – also for the first time: it was in the gangrene eating at the stump of a leg; it was aiming its vicious guns at her city; it was not in every breath you breathed. 'What a comment on the times we live in,' she whispered to the psychologist one day, 'that we're probably happier than we've ever been!' They were snatching a breath of fresh air, on one of the balconies. His mind still curing the head wound, as he gazed at the frozen river, he sighed and nodded.

He had thrown himself back into medical work, joyfully, and she was working directly under his orders. Elena learned from him, or from the few experienced nurses, or used her common sense. Love, she found, was an excellent medicine for dragging patients back from death, or helping them go into it peacefully. Love poured out of her and yet more came to take its place: a lake filled by an invisible stream. She carried the smells of gangrene and blood to her bed, where she was usually too tired to take off her clothes.

And twelve hours or so later, Michael would flop on to the same bed. Hospital and sleep. Sleep and hospital. No time or energy for anything else. He hadn't written anything for months. A poet always looks for a good excuse not to write; and this was the best excuse of all. His only diversion was an occasional brief walk in the garden with Elena, or sometimes with the psychologist.

He was with the latter now, sharing some bread and cheese in his room. He had come up during his midday break to have a talk on how they should deal with the horrifying new kind of injury: blindness induced by breathing poison gas; but instead, found himself engaged in a fascinating conversation about the sacred marriage of a man and his anima, the sun and the moon; at the same time enjoying the gooseberry wine the psychologist had bottled from last autumn's fruit crop in the garden. It was refreshing to break away for a time from the sufferings that surrounded them, and the psychologist was stimulating company, his mind leaping across chasms just as the poet's did. He sparkled; having a purpose in life again made him look twenty years younger.

They were interrupted by a tap on the door, and Elena walked in. The poet hadn't seen her, except in passing, for days. She was taken aback at finding him there, and flashed him a surprised and radiant smile, pushing her long fair hair back from her eyes in that gesture that was partly a habit, an expression of embarrassment or uncertainty. Seeing her, so unexpectedly, reminded Michael how always her image was present to him – when he operated, when he applied dressings, when he smiled hope and encouragement at a dying face, when he slept. Her appearance now, in the flesh, excited him and solaced him at once, because her beauty was so astonishing and yet so normal and ordinary. She was in a fresh white uniform, after a couple of hours' sleep, but hadn't yet donned her cap; her hair flowed free. Somehow her uniform made her seem taller, and gave her a slightly awkward, tense poise, like a caryatid. And her eyes – so direct and honest they might have looked straight into the sun. Her beauty, plain and without make-up, freshly washed, made his soul tremble, in a way that had little to do with how she looked. It was something more mysterious and more material.

The psychologist asked her to join them in the bread and cheese and homemade wine, and she sat on the bed. She too had come to discuss the blinded, shell-shocked soldiers. She hadn't been able to sleep a wink, worrying about them. Also she had had, she told them, an upsetting experience in the night. A boy of six, victim of a stray bomb, had died in her presence. He was not in any pain, and knew he was going to die. He had asked Elena, with wide and frightened eyes, what heaven was like. She had taken his hand and told him it was like a Christmas party, with lots of food and games and people who loved him, and a beautiful lit-up Christmas tree. He had smiled at this idea and his eyes lost their fear. She told him to hold her hand tight, close his eyes and count up to a hundred before opening them; and when he opened them he would find the loveliest and biggest Christmas present he had ever had.

Elena had tears in her eyes and her friends were not far from tears either. The psychologist spoke quietly about the psychological aspects of dying, then turned smoothly to the merits of the cheese, giving his nurse a chance to regain her composure; then he discussed with her, very professionally and yet caringly, a patient who was giving them cause for anxiety.

Although Michael was to some extent the odd man out he did not feel awkward or resentful. He drank the gooseberry wine quietly and looked out, from his seat near the window. The trees were in leaf and the canal was beginning to move its weight of ice. The distant gunfire could not mar the dull day's tranquil scene. He glanced from time to time at Elena, deep in conversation. He realized that his soul trembled before her image partly because he saw her as drawing away (as we see the stars) rather than drawing nearer. War had this effect; and perhaps this was as it should be, for him at least. He recognized his inability to love perfectly except when the eyes of wolves gleamed outside the window. Perfect love casteth out fear; but maybe, for him, fear was the only circumstance that could create perfect love.

As she talked to the psychologist, every gesture she made, every look she gave, every bite of her lip, every furrow of her brow, every absentminded stroke of her hair, every crossing of her legs, seemed both necessary and free – as Michael had once seen Peter draw a perfect circle with one bold movement of his hand.

The poet could feel, welling up inside him, an astonishing joy. This meaningless moment seemed alone meaningful. The chipped jug containing the sour wine held secrets unknown to Socrates. See, he was tipping the chipped jug and pouring the wine into Elena's chipped cup and some of it was splashing on to her lap! It was wonderful! A moment of utter clarity in which he saw God. The line of a poem came into his head: 'Are we, perhaps, *here* just for saying: House, Bridge, Fountain, Gate, Jug, Fruit tree, Window—'

The city's defenders were falling back, fighting every inch, a life for every stone. But some people said it was the enemy who was actually struggling and dying to bring them freedom; the tyrants were still inside. That cynical theory was too painful to believe, and Michael and Elena did not believe it.

Chapter Thirty-Five

She was dreaming about swimming naked in the sea, as a girl, out to that rock where she could lie and sunbathe all day, like the pure pagan she was, but worried lest the tramp stumble across her striped dress buried in the sand. The sun was sparkling off the cliffs and she was swimming lazily. She started to cough. It was nothing, some sea water had gone down her throat; but the cough got worse as she neared the rock, and it was so bad it woke her up.

The room was full of smoke. Choking, she swung her legs out of bed: pushed past the obstructing blanket and pulled open the window. Gulping air, she saw people down in the street. They were staring up, shouting, waving their arms. Quickly she pulled on her shoes and ran to the door. A blast of heat and smoke drove her back. Flames filled the corridor to the right, roaring, devouring the rotten wood.

It was never found for sure how the fire had started. They traced it to the laundry room on Elena's corridor. It could have been arson — perhaps a matchbox bomb hidden among the clothes. Or it could have been Elena's former mistress, whose remains were found there. Maybe she had been smoking, or deliberately set fire to herself. Anyway, it was a wonder it had not happened earlier: for the house was a fire trap.

Someone shouted to Elena from along the corridor to her left, and she stumbled towards his voice. Now she remembered there was a fire escape along there. She saw a strip of daylight, and some figures crowding up to it to get through. The man who had called to her seized her arm and asked her if she was okay. She nodded, gasping, recovering her breath. They must wait their turn: there were others scrambling down the escape ladder from higher floors. The smoke was thicker, choking, the flames nearer. Where were the fucking extinguishers? the man snarled.

There was a gap in the endless press of bodies on the fire escape. It was his turn, then hers. He swung on to the ladder and held out his hand to her. But Elena had run back into the black smoke, holding her hand to her mouth, trying not to breathe. She kept to the wall, feeling for the door knobs; it would be the only way she could know when she had reached her own room – by the particular grain on her door. She came to it, the heat engulfing her now, and she could see the flames that roared and crackled in her eardrums. She edged forward to the next door. The knob was so hot she could not turn it, but she pushed the door with her shoulder and it opened.

Choking, holding on to sense by a thread, she crouched down on hands and knees to try to find some air. Air was suddenly the dearest thing in the world. She kicked the door shut behind her and crawled across the room, searching in the smoke. At last she found the girl, lying in the corner, curled up small. She was unconscious, perhaps dead. Elena staggered to her feet, and fumbled with the window catch. When it would not give, she picked up a chair, and battered the window open, glass and wood splintering together. She retched, and heaved air into her lungs. She dragged the girl back to the door, but opening it an inch was like opening the door of a furnace, and she slammed it shut. She dragged the girl back to the window, and pulled her up so that her head was draped across the sill. A blazing man plunged from the sky past the window. Elena pulled her head away sharply.

Now there were people down there, in white coats. They were staring up at her and shouting. Now they were standing in a circle under the window, stretching out a blanket. They wanted her to jump. She shut her eyes, shook her head. She had always been terrified of heights.

She could see the doctors' mouths framing the word 'jump' but she could only hear the flames. She pulled the girl up till her stomach was resting on the sill, her head hanging down towards the street. Holding on to her firmly with one hand, Elena swung herself out on to the sill. She poised there a moment, her eyes closed; then in a reflex way tucked the hem of her uniform under her thighs. Very slowly, careful not to overtopple, she dragged the girl towards her until she was clasped in her arms, her legs still dangling in the room. She looked down at the swaying street, guessed the thrust necessary to land in the blanket, held the girl with all her strength, tensed her muscles, thrust her feet against the bricks and sailed off down through the air.

Chapter Thirty-Six

The poetess came back with no news of her nephew. She had found the town of her birth in ruins. The house where the widow had lived no longer existed. Someone said he had seen a middle-aged woman and a boy – who appeared to resemble their nephew – walking along the road, out of town, carrying a suitcase and a bundle. They might be anywhere or nowhere. Finding no way of getting back to the city, Marion had put up in the room of a childhood friend, helped to dig out the dead and the living and to get the pulse of the town beating again, however feebly. The town changed hands several times. She had asked everyone she met if they had seen a woman with a boy, and everyone had reacted by laughing.

The three friends were living now in an attic, previously used as a store-room, next to the janitor's. When it was cleared out and cleaned up it was quite roomy, but it had no window. The naked skylight was huge and rather frightening. In summer it would make the room unbearably hot, just as now, in winter, it was icy; the small electric fire merely took the edge off the frost; most of the time they stayed in their coats. They hated not being able to look out, felt out of touch with the earth. It was all very well being able to look up at the moon and stars: even poets could have too much of that. Elena missed looking out at the maple tree. The best that could be said for the room was that it let in more light.

There was no chance of going back to the other room. The whole wing was gutted. Their few possessions had gone up in smoke. 'So what!' said Marion, shrugging.

The armies had made a truce. The enemy held all the city and land to the south of the river. The authorities on the north were proclaiming a great defensive victory, and the people felt weary but hopeful. Nothing, said the press and radio, would be too good for the disbanding soldiers. And truly, already in Elena's house officials had been checking what would be needed in the empty hospital wards to turn them into a fit home for blinded heroes.

Elena had found a job as an assistant in the dress department of a large store. She enjoyed meeting people and doing her best to send them away pleased. She counted her blessings. Her burns had healed, leaving practically no scars; her collar bone and ankle bone had mended perfectly. She had survived, and so had her friends. The last war of all time, so people said, had ended. There would be freedom and fair shares. Who could complain about a skylight instead of a window?

On the last day of January, the three of them went to the new cemetery tucked away in a bend of the river. They were struck dumb by its endlessness and uniformity. Elena, who had come once before with the psychologist, placed a bunch of snowdrops on the grave of the crippled girl she had tried to rescue, and another on the grave of the little boy who had opened his eyes to the beautiful Christmas present. Then they stood silently mourning all the dead, known and unknown, friend and enemy, for 'the dead are all on the same side'. From this high ground they could see the cathedral dome and the city's towers. Though it had two names now, to their eyes it was one city; severed only by the winding frozen river – that is, no more than is the flesh of lovers. And tomorrow would be St Valentine's Day. There was to be a two-week break in the calendar, for some obscure reason – for the sake of uniformity, it was said. But people had had enough of uniforms, and did not appreciate losing two weeks of their lives.

What, asked the poet, should they do with themselves in these fourteen white days? Maybe they would live in a proper house, with a proper husband or wife, and two proper children; with time and energy for proper love affairs and divorces and heartbreaks! The people who had these things already – didn't they realize how lucky they were? His sister was silent, like a nun in her blacks. Perhaps she had too many people to mourn and too little time. Or perhaps there is something of this moment in her later poem which contains the lines 'I, like a river, have been turned aside by this harsh age . . .' and 'Life is a place where it's forbidden/to live' – that poem which ends by saying that if her *un*deflected self could look at her, as she was now, she would at last know the meaning of envy. Because, like her friend's collar bone and ankle bone broken in the fall, she was the stronger for the breaks.

Who can refuse to live his own life?

Elena was going to a St Valentine's Eve dance at the Arts Theatre. Her companions had cried off, and she was left to go alone with the psychologist. Not that she minded that; they were really good friends; he was cultured and polite. She was only worried that he might not enjoy it. At his age, he might think it too frivolous. But he joined in merrily enough with the bright, meaningless chatter, and admired the tasteless décor: the walls covered with technicolour blow-ups of romantic scenes from the movies. There was an excellent jazz band; Elena dragged her grey-haired friend on to the dance floor; he shuffled amiably, and smiled at her as she kicked and jiggled to the lively music. After all, she was young, and still alive, and wearing a shimmery sort of lilac dress which felt good on her. The manager had let her buy it for a song, because it was slightly imperfect and because of her unfailing smile. The frock was tight over the chest but then belled out, and came to above her knees – she felt very daring! And she had bought some pearls – well, not exactly pearls – and had had her hair cut in a kind of page-boy style, since she liked Marion's fringe and was tired of long hair.

They drank the bubbly, and he lurched around as she jived, and they talked to friends. Some of the girls from her cancan days were there, with their husbands or boyfriends; and so, of course, was the gay impresario, greyer, and with one jacket sleeve in his pocket, but elegantly casual in his blazer and blue silk cravat, and drawling jokes from the side of his long black ciagarette holder. He was curious – as who was not? – about the nature of the sharing that was going on between Elena and the poets. '*Who* exactly sleeps with *whom*?' he drawled, with a lift of his brows. But Elena laughingly and adroitly turned the subject. Later she was to say, to one of her closest friends, that she had never slept with the poet, 'in the fullest sense'.

The poet was in bed — half-awake — alone — when he caught scuffling sounds coming from next door. A full moon shone through the skylight, and he was able to look at his watch: midnight. Elena was no Cinderella; they would not have got back from the dance. A lot of thieving had been taking place; in almost everyone, moral values had been damaged by the war; he thought he ought to investigate. Putting on his army greatcoat over his pyjamas, he crept past his sister (her eyes were shut, but she lay fully awake, on the heights of insomnia), opened the door to the dark landing, poised himself — threw open the door and clicked the light. Elena was on the bed, naked except for her pink elastic roll-on, which the naked psychologist was attempting to pull off and she was pretending to be struggling to keep on. The poet muttered an apology, switched out the light, and shut the door.

Chapter Thirty-Seven

He used the bucket, climbed back into his bed, and stared up at the moon. He caught the faint noise of streetwalkers, far below, singing, laughing, and chanting slogans as they passed the house. He heard the great cathedral bell toll one. He looked at his wristwatch and it said twelve. He shook the watch, looked at it again, put his arm back under the blanket and lay still.

The moon looked at him.

'He waited for the dawn, but there was no dawn.'

The poetess thought he had spoken, and she spoke his name, questioningly. He did not answer.

A large black cat was sitting on the skylight. It had long whiskers, and its eyes gleamed in the moonlight. It grinned at the poet, and closed its left eye in a wink. The round yellow moon became a cheese on the black velvet tablecloth. The cat winked at him again and, opening its jaws wide, took a huge chunk out of the moon.

Chapter Thirty-Eight

Marion sniffed the air one day and caught an unmistakable odour. As we know from her lyric, dust smells of a sun ray, and girls' mouths smell of apples, but blood smells only of blood. It was not for nothing that her brother called her Cassandra. The situation suddenly grew much worse, grew unspeakable. In comparison, all the past repressions seemed like the caress of a velvet glove.

The theatrical director wanted to do something to help Michael. He had a word with his friend the choreographer, and they came up with the idea of asking him to write a children's pantomime. Nothing could be more harmless than that. The director telephoned a friend who telephoned a friend who knew someone with influence, and at last the director was given permission to approach Michael. He had gratefully accepted, and now he had invited them round, two months before the New Year, to hear the first draft of his script. Marion, Elena and the psychologist were also present. The poet had chosen Dick Whittington as his theme, and had written the script in funny rhyming couplets which children would enjoy. He read all the parts, and had his friends in a constant chuckle – at a time when laughter was scarcer than green figs.

But there was one scene, funnier and more brilliant than the rest, which was heard in silence. The Devil is annoyed because a certain city has gained the reputation of being wickeder than Hell. With his assistant (a beautiful girl witch in a black cat suit) he visits the city and they impersonate Dick and his cat while those two heroes lie in a drugged sleep. The Devil, a very good-humoured fellow, turns the tables on the cruel grocer by revealing to all the customers that the tins of catmeat on special offer for the New Year actually contain, not horsemeat, but human flesh. The customers beat the grocer with umbrellas and walking sticks, because everybody knows that human flesh can be got dirt cheap, and the grocer is grossly over-charging.

The blubbering grocer has no excuse to offer except that the Lord Mayor has forced him to buy all the inferior meat from the city abattoir. The grocer's exposure of the wicked Mayor leaves the way clear, of course, for the election of Dick Whittington.

The director and the one-armed choreographer, their faces a greenish colour, said they liked most of the material but there were some parts that weren't suitable for children. But when Michael struck a match and set light to the offending section, saying this part was only a private joke between friends, they cheered up; the director put his hand to his mouth, snorted, laughed outright, the choreographer slapped his leg with his good hand, threw his head back and cackled. The psychologist grinned hugely, taking off his glasses and rubbing them. It was a wonderful scene, they all agreed, and what a shame it could not be included. The director, composing his face as he stood to leave, asked Michael to get busy with the final script and to bring it to him in a week.

That same night, Elena and Marion were awake in the same instant as they heard the hum of a motor and the slam of a car door. They held their breaths, praying it was one of the highly placed security officials who lived in the large apartments, back late after important business. Then, when they heard footsteps mounting the stairs in their part of the house, they hoped (for the flesh is weak) that the steps would stop below their level and the knock would be on someone else's door. But this time the footsteps did not stop, but got louder and louder, and nearer and nearer, and the fists hammered on their door.

And there, behind the two security police, was the pale-faced psychologist, wearing, as it were, his janitor's hat. In the morning, when Elena and the poetess were there alone, he was to come into their room again, and cry.

It was useless trying to ask themselves which of their friends could have betrayed the poet. People did these things, not because they were evil, but under extreme pressure. It was absolute folly of Michael to have burdened them with such a temptation. You could only talk in whispers, at night, under the bedclothes, to your wife . . . And sometimes not even then.

Michael, sitting in his cell, was curious that he felt so resigned. He was grateful that they had not found the slim book Elena had sewn into his jacket lining, a book so small that only a man with his keen sight could have read from it. He had been living a posthumous life. For at least a day he actually believed Elena had betrayed him, slipping out in the dark to telephone. He believed this, not for any logical reason, but because he had seen his death in the night sky, and felt it in his innermost being, and she was closely bound up with both.

He admitted everything, at his first interrogation. By an odd concession to legality, the verbatim record of the questioning still exists in the files and can be inspected. Some of the most interesting exchanges occurred very early on (while most of the city slept in, for it was a Sunday).

'You admit to being the poet of that name?'

'Not in this room. I'm not anything unless I'm free.'

'Have you had intercourse with foreigners?'

'Yes.'

'Who were they?'

'A half-caste cinema usherette and some angels.'

'Have you been passing on information?'

'No, but they have shared some of their secrets with me.'

There followed a confused exchange in which the poet said the cinema usherette concealed secrets in her vagina and the interrogator tried to establish whether they were in the form of microfilm.

'Do you admit that you have allowed some of your work to be published in hostile countries, countries whose political and social systems are designed to oppress the people?'

'I have published in this country, yes.'

'How much longer do we have to proceed like this?'

'To the very grave, woman.'

The poet was forced to explain that he was quoting the Archpriest Avvakum, in response to his exhausted wife who asked how much further they must go.

'Do you admit to publishing a poem expressing crudely hostile feelings towards the authorities?'

'My poems acknowledge only one authority?'

'Who is that?'

'Cinema usherettes.'

'Aren't you disgracing your profession by offering these absurdities?'

'No, it's the truth. They shine a light in darkness. Why is that man screaming?'

'You can't make an omelette without breaking eggs.'

'But human beings are not eggs and you haven't made an omelette but a hash.'

His interlocutor returned to the question of his espionage. 'Angels' was clearly a code name; did he admit this? Yes. Did he admit they were spies, contacts? Yes. Where had he met them? In all-night cinemas, bars, railway waiting rooms, public lavatories, parks, buses.

The interrogation moved to a statement Michael had made in an interview, an admission that he used invisible ink.

'Do any of these secret communications still exist?'

'Yes. There are some in the book you're holding. Incidentally, I don't know *why* you're holding it. I don't have one and I've never seen it. All the copies were destroyed in the printing house. It is very dangerous for you to hold it. I beg you to give it to me.'

There was a break at this point while the book was sent for laboratory analysis and doubtless the interrogator had a cup of coffee. When discussion resumed the poet was reprimanded for wasting time: the book contained no messages in invisible ink. The poet referred to a poem in which a swan ravishes a girl. That was in invisible ink, he said.

'Tell me what it says.'

'It says we shall always be saved from ourselves.'

'By foreign interventionists?'

'Yes.'

'What's the meaning of this line: "I hold my word tight to my breast"? What word is that? Is that your code word?'

'Yes.'

'What *is* it?'

'Truth.'

'Does that mean you also have a contact at that newspaper?'

'Yes.'

'Who?'

'The whole lot.'

'The whole lot?'

'Yes, they're all foreign agents.'

'All of them?'

'All the reporters and editorial staff, yes.'

The transcript indicates that from this moment the poet 'coughed' non-stop. He confessed that the editorial departments of radio and television were likewise riddled with traitors, as were the history and literature departments of the university and the teachers' college. Most stunning of all (though his interrogator does not register particular surprise) was his admission that many of his contacts belonged to the secret police.

He also betrayed more than two dozen persons by name from Akhnaton to Zola.

Later that same day, the day of the arrest, while Elena was out in the silent streets trying to get word of her friend's whereabouts, a man in a fur coat puffed up to their room and offered the poetess a travel warrant, for herself and her girlfriend. There was not much time, he said. The poetess thanked him and sent him away.

Chapter Thirty-Nine

Through the usual grapevine, Elena found out the name of the prison. Then she went to the cathedral, which was sometimes opened for two hours on a Sunday, but the doors were locked. Coming back, she bumped into her department boss, out walking with his mistress. A genial fellow, he stopped to pass the time of day. Times were bad, he sighed, and he had heard he would have to lay off staff. Unfortunately Elena ... He sighed again, and slipped a banknote into her coat pocket.

As soon as she heard the name of the prison, Marion pulled her coat on and dashed out. Elena heard a whisper on the stairs, and then the tap-tap of a stick coming up as Marion's feet clattered down. It was Peter. She helped him towards the chair – though he was terribly proud and independent. They talked in whispers, miserably. Life was bad for him too. The shell that had blinded him kept on exploding. He was having to beg at street corners, though he knew for a fact that two or three of his portraits, of Elena or of his wife, had sold for huge sums in the special shops. He was learning to draw again, though. He had brought his sketch pad with him, and asked her if he could do her portrait. She let him run his hand over her face, and then, feeling for the edges of his sheet, he drew some rapid lines. When he had finished he asked her, nervously, what she thought. She looked at his drawing and swallowed a lump in her throat. Her face was not together but in separate fragments, an eye here, a nose there. But she told him it was good. 'No,' he said, 'but it will be.'

Every day thereafter, for several months, in snow and in heat, the poetess joined the queue which – if someone had given all the orphans and widows in it a rifle – would have made the biggest army in history. Most of the time Elena came with her, and the two women became even closer. They regarded themselves as sisters. 'There are four of us,' Marion whispered (for everyone in the queue whispered); by which Elena understood she meant herself and Elena, and Michael and their brother Joseph. When they eventually reached the little window, the barking guard never had any news for them, and would never accept the food parcel; but back they would come the next day, in case. At night when they lay down to converse with their insomnia, their breasts felt like rocks.

One day a frozen-faced woman in a ragged coat recognized the poetess (though she had greatly changed), and whispered to the tall beautiful girl with the bad cough, standing beside her, and she in turn whispered to the man in front; until people all along the line were looking round and giving Marion the shadow of a smile; and Elena asked the tall girl why they were doing this, and she whispered, 'Because they know she will bear witness when the time comes.'

The poetess wept when she heard this; but from that moment she seemed to get stronger and stronger (though both were enduring another spell of 'clinical starvation'), as if she was drawing strength from these humble and weak people, as if someone was going up the line with a hat and each person was dropping a coin in, for her. Only it was not a coin, but a fragment of their strength. She wrote a sequence of poems, 'The Witness', which she never wrote down, but simply recited to Elena. Even Elena had no trouble in understanding it, and it brought tears to her eyes.

Chapter Forty

Except for those unknown friends, they were very much on their own. Peter occasionally tapped his way to their room, but apart from him they had few visitors. Few wanted to risk contamination by associating with foreign elements – to be blunt: spies. Judging by the number of arrests, you would think that every night droves of enemy agents covered their faces in boot black to swim stealthily across the river, before losing themselves in the streets and houses. If a lifelong friend or neighbour was arrested, people would exclaim, 'Thank God he's been found out in time!'

Apart from each man's natural instinct to cling on to his own piece of driftwood, the authorities had discovered another infallible method of ensuring a minimum of trouble. This was really a stroke of genius; and it is said that when this droll scheme was first mooted in the council chamber, the deputies laughed spontaneously – the only time this has occurred – laughed until they cried. The device was to label everything 'the People's'. Every object or institution, from prunes to prisons, became 'the People's'. Thus, if people thought themselves to be – or patently were – duped, wronged, oppressed, tormented, by this or that, they could not complain because they would be complaining against the People – that is, themselves. If they felt, as they all did, that some monster was lying on top of them and choking the life out of them, they could not struggle to fight him off, because the monster was the People – themselves. Many people were driven crazy by this logical conundrum and, not bothering to wait for the People's justice, blew their brains out.

At night, when all the arrests happened, the two women stood watch like soldiers. If a car stopped outside, if there was the tramp of boots up the stairs, one was always awake to shake the other by the shoulder. If it came to them, they wanted to be awake and alert; they had a horror of stumbling around still half-asleep, while uncouth fingers went through their belongings and uncouth voices bullied them to get a move on. While Elena took each day as being sufficiently evil, Marion foresaw their arrest, foresaw how it would happen in the clearest possible detail, and admitted to being petrified every moment of the day and night. Strength and courage did not imply a lack of that 'holy terror' she admitted to feeling. She refers to these torturing nights in the line: 'Fear and the Muse take turns at watch.'

They saw little of the psychologist. He may not have been deliberately keeping out of their way: he was kept so busy at night that by day he had to sleep a lot. Elena was glad she did not see much of him. The possibility that he was Judas, even a reluctant Judas, made her bitterly regret her affair with him.

But he did come in to see them one day, after he had got beaten up in the street. They sympathized in moderation, and Elena bathed his bruises. And they could not help feeling genuinely sorry for him when he came again, a week later, to tell them he was leaving the house, he had been ordered to go somewhere else. He was white, sure he would never see them again; he carried his death warrant in his eyes and, though they did their best to cheer him up, in their hearts they knew that his death was upon him – him, and many thousands of others. They had heard the order over the radio.

The order related to a building that looked like an old fortress or perhaps a dilapidated football stadium, in the least fashionable inner suburb. It had housed the slaves who had built the city and later worked in the silver mines to the north.

You sailed up the grandest canal. You did not land with the rest of the passengers to stroll through the triumphal gate and down the famous avenue of limes – you went on for one more stage and landed on the opposite bank. You walked north along narrow, rank-smelling canals, between derelict factories and warehouses, till you came to this slum of slums. Here the narrow canal turned into a moat encircling the 'fortress'. There were three bridges leading to openings in the blank wall. You might expect it to be alive with football supporters at three o'clock of a Saturday. But if curiosity carried you inside, you would have found a dusty, stony arena, surrounded by rotting tenements. You would not want to stay long.

Known as the ghetto, it had housed Jews after the emancipation of the slaves. They could leave to run their businesses by day, and might even grow rich, but at night they had to return here, under strict curfew. Now, thank God, the ghetto was all but deserted. A few tramps, gypsies, meths drinkers, down-and-outs of various kinds, dossed here from time to time, that was all. Those apart, it was occupied by rats: literally millions of rats.

It was an eyesore, a cancer spot. No self-respecting city could tolerate it. And at last something was being done. The meths drinkers and bums were quietly disposed of. Then came the general order which had caused the psychologist, and thousands of others, to start packing. It said that since Jews had been harassed recently by unruly elements they were requested, for their own security, to remove themselves to the ghetto and abide by a six o'clock curfew. This regrettable move would be only temporary; the authorities knew the accommodation was sadly inadequate. Work studies had already been set under way to find a satisfactory long-term solution. Every citizen with the letter J at the end of his social security number (this was the number people carried tattooed on their wrists as a precaution against infiltrators) should report to the ghetto, carrying no more than one suitcase, by six o'clock.

The grey-headed psychologist shambled off with his case, and the next day a fresh-faced, thuggish youth with cropped hair moved in next door. Through a chink of her door Elena watched him make several trips downstairs, his arms loaded with books. On his last trip he went down with a petrol can. 'For angels rent the house next ours ...' she whispered to Marion ironically. They fell silent with shame. They knew they ought to have stepped outside, demanded to know what he was doing with someone else's property. But they were afraid.

That night, the poetess was sitting in the dark, waiting. She heard the sound of an engine, and grew tense. It was a long way off; everyone's hearing had become exceptional. Then she realized it came from the sky, and she relaxed. But she did not sleep; it was a close night; there was thunder. In the morning the radio announcer wore an unusually grave voice. It had been necessary to bomb the ghetto with high explosives. The ghetto, it had been found, was riddled with bubonic plague. Already deaths had occurred on the mainland, but the outbreak, thanks to this immediate, tragic but unavoidable action, could be contained. The alternative would have been a death rate amounting to millions. The remains of the ghetto would be fumigated, razed to the ground, and turned into a garden shrine to those who had sacrificed their lives for the people. The radio carried funeral music for the rest of the morning, interspersed with bulletins re-emphasizing the deadly peril that had been averted by prompt and courageous action. 'The most heart-rending decision of my entire life,' the responsible minister had said mournfully.

Marion and Elena had lost friends in this holocaust. They spent the next three days rushing around scrounging money from better-off friends so that they could push banknotes under the pillows of others who had lost their breadwinner. Marion was also struggling to write a poem, vaguely in her brother's style, that would please the authorities. She could say, 'Look at this,' and — who knows? — they might release him. It was indescribable torture trying to write a bad poem in a style that could pass for Michael's. If it worked, she prayed God he would forgive her.

Elena started to work again at the Arts Theatre, now an intimate cabaret for high-ranking officers of the armed forces. For themselves, they could exist on air, but now there was a third mouth to feed. One June evening, having dragged home from the prison in utter exhausted despair — they had at last been told that Michael had gone, weeks ago, to one of the camps — they found a woman cowering in their room. They knew her only slightly, a quiet, melancholy woman, wife of the theatrical director. He had been killed in the ghetto, but she had escaped the bombs and had also been left for dead, under a pile of corpses, when the troops had come in to mop up. During the night she had made her escape and had been hiding ever since. She was starving as well as terrified, and she knew that Elena and the poetess were good women. Would they shelter her? She was sure she did not have the plague, and Elena and Marion believed her.

She would be reasonably safe if she kept absolutely quiet, since the young thug next door left them alone. He seemed to be afraid of women — twice he had bumped into one or other of them and had literally scuttled away. If, at night, they heard the first sounds of danger, she had time to climb up through the skylight and hide on the roof. She would still have a chance even if the others were taken. The added risk and hardship of the woman's presence actually cheered the poetess up. 'We are at our best defending something,' she said, and shrugged.

So Elena went to see the gay choreographer. He was frightened to be seen talking to her, but had problems of his own. Two of his best girls had been lost in the defensive action against the plague, and his customers liked only the best. Elena's record was bad, but at least she was not a Jewess. He wanted very much to help her and Marion if he dared. 'Can you sing?' he asked; and she said she could. He would take a chance. He didn't think the officers would make too many inquiries so long as they could ogle a beautiful girl – and Elena, though she was very thin, was still beautiful. Yes, he would give her a break. He asked her to try on the outfit of one of the dead girls, and it fitted.

Her act was a hit with the jackbooted officers and their dolled-up women. Coins and even notes rained on to the stage. She had to come on dressed in black: black tailored suit, black boots, black gloves, a rakish black hat, nicely set off by a frilly white blouse. Singing a dreamy, alluring song, she stripped, very slowly, her outer garments. Dressed in the high, high-heeled boots, black stockings, black suspender belt, black briefs, black brassière, and long black gloves, she paused in her song to sit down and take a packet of cigarettes – black cigarettes – and a black holder, from her handbag. Languidly she lit the cigarette. Then she stood again to sing in her husky tones between languid puffs. She could feel the aching lust all over the room. By the time she had reached the stage of unclipping her brassière, the officers' fat necks were swelling around their tight collars like the cork in a champagne bottle.

She hated her act because she hated her audience. But so far, her trickiest moments were in fobbing off admirers at the dressing-room door. Then one afternoon the one-armed impresario asked her to rehearse a novelty in her act. He had allowed his kindness to get the better of him again. When an old soldier in dark glasses, a poison gas victim, came to him begging for a job, what could he say? Besides, the man had an impeccable pass card, was an experienced actor, and also seemed sexually rather promising. The man was a specialist in 'drag' roles, very popular at the time.

Elena's boss told her he wanted to try her out in a double act, with a new girl he had hired.

She was instructed in what to do when her new partner came on stage. When she reached the cigarette-lighting pause, a girl who looked like her double sidled on to the stage – also wearing black boots, black stockings, black gloves, etc., and smoking a black cigarette in a black holder. The only real difference was that she was a little taller and broader, and wore dark glasses. The impresario couldn't resist a little clap from the wings, and even the bored musicians and the empty auditorium seemed attentive.

The act proceeded according to plan. The other girl, her double, joined her in the continued song – she had a lighter voice – and then the two girls embraced, danced a few steps, kissed and fondled each other. The double removed Elena's brassière and fondled her breasts. Elena felt uncomfortable being stroked by gloves, having to gaze into the heavily made-up face – like a white mask – and having to kiss the clinging, scarlet lips. She would have preferred an erotic act with a man, but this . . . She sat in the chair while the girl pulled off Elena's high boots; then stood to let her peel off her gloves, stockings, and all her clothes till she was naked. They sang again, arms round each other. At the conclusion, as a *coup de théâtre*, Elena's double lifted her blond wig off, to expose a close-cropped head.

The impresario watched Elena's shocked reaction with amusement. It was a good joke – and it really showed that his new performer could do his stuff. What he could not know was that Elena had suddenly recognized the gentle old lady who had rescued her from the rapist. The transvestite took off his glasses – his eyes were scarred but by no means sightless – leered at his partner knowingly, and winked.

Chapter Forty-One

Elena had never been good at sums, but in the next weeks and months she was to become an expert at rapid mental arithmetic. She could tell instantly how many people a cattle truck could hold, at the limit, everyone jammed together, standing, and how many were actually being pushed inside before the doors were slammed shut. She also found out something more about her body, something she had never learned as a nurse: the tyrannical power of the respiratory system to force one's body to stay erect, no matter who else got trampled underfoot.

In the camp, she knew at once exactly how many would be left without boots and without coats, and therefore how many would freeze to death before nightfall.

When the doctor had already extracted the dying, the sick, and the feeble, the camp guards sometimes chose at random – say every third or fourth or fifth woman – to make up the day's quota. At these times, she knew at once which number she was in the line, and instantly divided that by the appropriate numeral.

One icy morning, it was not yet dawn, she knew she was the ninety-third woman in the line and that they were selecting every fourth woman. But the prisoner on her right, the ninety-second, a small hump-backed woman who had been a mathematics graduate, started to shake, as if she had a high fever. Although Elena clung to life because she might be the only person alive to preserve the poets' writings (she had lost sight of Marion soon after their arrest), it suddenly became clear to her that all the poetry in the world could not equal this terrified, shaking woman. It was greater than her, but also less. It was only greater inasmuch as it recognized that it was less than this woman. So Elena, without a second thought, took her arm and changed places with her in the line. But when the officer came level and was about to tap Elena on the shoulder, he recoiled slightly. He was new to this post, his powers of observation not yet completely blunted, and somehow he recognized, in this skeletal figure wearing a ragged coat and hobnailed boots, the beautiful leather-booted strip artist at the cabaret back home. He tapped the hunchback instead – she stumbled forward without a murmur – and ordered Elena to stay behind while the rest were dismissed to their work parties.

Put to serve in the officers' brothel, fattened up like a goose for Christmas, Elena made a point of pleasing the young captain so well that she could demand a favour. She asked him to find out if a certain poet had come to this camp, and if so, what had happened to him. At last the captain, as a reward for a particularly pleasant session, told her that her friend had indeed been in this camp, but he had passed through very quickly to freedom. The records indicated that he had died of a heart attack. Using all her artful promises, she persuaded him to question the stool pigeons in the men's section, and eventually she discovered which hut he had lived in. One of the stool pigeons recalled an old man who had spouted poetry after lights-out to a group of prisoners. It had been all double dutch to him, but one of the titles was 'Christmas Star' and he had been going to report him for using bourgeois terminology. But the old man had died in the night.

While the prisoners were out working, Elena made the stool

pigeon take her to the very bunk in which he had died. Some words had been scratched, probably with a nail, in the wood, near where his head had rested: 'the patient is no longer here'. Elena was sure he had written these words, and she committed them to memory as his last poem, or fragment.

Now that the poet's work was finished, she tried hard to picture it as a whole. There were black spells when nothing seemed to matter, poetry least of all. She desperately needed something she could see and grasp, to boost her sense that she must stay alive (though not at any price). At first she saw a fat and sumptuous book. But the poems were not there. The contents might just as well be about ice skating or sugar making. The image she needed was given her, unexpectedly, by a baby.

For — talking of Christmas stars — there was a baby in the brothel. God knows how, or why, it had survived the countless pogroms, natural and manmade, but there it was. Whores who got pregnant were allowed to go their full term because one of the senior officers enjoyed pregnant women. Apart from a number of miscarriages, there had been five full-term pregnancies. Two babies had been still-born, one had been destroyed at birth, and one had been kept alive for a year in the camp hospital's experimental unit. The fifth baby was allowed to live and stay with his mother because he had been born on the Leader's birthday, and at the very same hour.

Nearly a year old, he slept in a cubicle next to his mother's. A lively, inquisitive child, he crawled around everywhere, and his fingers were in everything. Strangely, he was happy and contented. Naturally, all the girls doted on him; he was the light in their darkness. They fought to have their turn at looking after him when his mother was working, and they spoiled him terribly. And yet he remained unspoiled. He was affectionate, but didn't like too much squeezing and hugging. He seemed to prefer those, like his mother and Elena, who loved him without squeezing him to death.

His mother complained that he simply wouldn't go to sleep. She would put him in his cot at seven, and he'd still be open-eyed at eight o'clock, at nine o'clock! He didn't cry, just lay there curled up awake, and he'd smile at you if you went in. She suspected that too many of her friends were creeping in, during breaks, to have a look, and they were disturbing him. But one of the older women said, with a far-away expression, that babies set their own sleep patterns, and there was nothing you could do about it, or should do, as long as they were healthy and happy.

Elena crept in one night, not to disturb the child but just to have a little peep. In the semi-darkness she saw his wide-open eyes. He was sucking his thumb, and he gave a little smile when he caught sight of her. Then he pulled himself up the bars, to take her finger in his and to have a little chat. He tried out some of his words, now addressing them to Elena and now to the picture of a sailing ship on the wall. He cooed and chuckled, and then settled down again, thumb in mouth. She adjusted the blanket around him, and he grinned at her, bright as a button. What thoughts, what pictures, what memories, went through his mind all these hours he lay awake? It was the most innocent, the most moving, the most profound, the most mysterious and beautiful thing in the whole world: his face, silently awake in his cot.

Whenever, by day, her eyes were dragged back to the belching chimneys (they waited for her too), she was glad that her friend had escaped into the free air. He had 'turned into the life-giving ear of grain,/And into the gentlest rain of which he sang' – these words came to her mysteriously, in a woman's voice, though they were not to be written until long after. But his poems were still here, and they too were free. For now, instead of seeing them as a fat and sumptuous book, she saw them as a baby's face, smiling in his own life in the half-dark cubicle under the picture of the sailing ship.

Chapter Forty-Two

Now that the fighting had resumed, every strong pair of patriotic hands was needed. Those prisoners who still had flesh on their bones were separated from the others. The whores (and one fretful baby) left their flimsy clothes in a changing room and were herded into a bath house. As if by an unspoken agreement they chatted brightly, so as not to upset the baby. Each girl in turn came up to kiss him, and then the hot water was turned on. Outside, to their surprise, were fresh clothes, and an empty cattle train. Elena found herself back in the city, and wearing khaki.

First one side had forced a bridgehead, and then the other; the battle swung through ninety degrees. Street by street, canal by canal, the city was contested. Before, no mercy had been shown in terms of human lives, but by an unspoken agreement the city's architectural glories were spared. Now shells, bombs and rockets crashed indiscriminately into churches, museums, art galleries, schools, hospitals. Fires burned for weeks all over the city.

The cathedral dome was shattered.

But the morale of the people held firm. Now it was 'the people' indeed. They did not count the cost. Even as they died, they would hand on to their children and their grandchildren their most precious possession, the language.

Elena was assigned to work in an operations room, deep underground. There was a huge round table, with a detailed map of the city and its environs. Her duty was to shift around the little coloured tanks, according to the colonel's instructions. The room was always choked with tension and bustle. Joy and despondency alternated, and all according to where her croupier's stick shifted the toy tanks. She worked till she dropped: ate and slept and entirely breathed the basement room. When she climbed up into the street for some fresh air she hardly knew if it was dawn or dusk. She shed a few tears when she saw the shattered dome. Yet someone got into the ancient building that had been locked for so long and actually pealed the bell! People stopped whatever they were doing, startled, wondering, and then cheered and lifted their caps into the air. Nothing would break their spirit!

The hospitals could not cope with the number of wounded. Elena volunteered to do nursing, and was delighted to find herself working again in the old house, sharing a room with four other good-hearted nurses. They were hardly ever in their room, so the overcrowding scarcely mattered. The wounds were different now; there were a lot of burn cases, brought about by that dreadful weapon the flame thrower. Later, more sinister, there were burns from radiation. Elena sometimes had to tend men and women and children who had had all their skin burnt off, a form of striptease that only war throws up to any great extent.

The time came when the defenders were entirely cut off. There was no food. People ate rats, and rats ate people. It looked as if the house itself might be overrun. Despite the warnings that anyone captured by the enemy would be raped and killed, Elena volunteered to stay behind with the patients who could not walk.

She had a special reason for volunteering to do this. More and more of the brave soldiers being brought in, hideously maimed, were mere boys – lads of fourteen or fifteen. It tore the heart to look at them. They ought to have been flying a kite or collecting engine numbers, not in a blood-soaked uniform, on a stretcher, their eyes haunted and questioning. One of these boy soldiers, his chest and face badly burnt, worried at Elena's memory. As his face healed she became sure that this was the boy she had taken to the zoo and the circus – the poet's nephew – even though the name on his pass book was unfamiliar. When he was able to talk, her belief was confirmed. He did not, of course, recognize Elena at once; but when she mentioned their trips to the zoo – the funny faces they had made up – his face brightened with recollection.

By desperate, suicidal courage, the line was held, two streets and two canals from the house.

When the boy was well enough to leave his bed, Elena asked the medical officer, who had a bit of a soft spot for her, if there was any chance of her being allotted a room of her own, or even half a room, so that she could look after her nephew until he could return to his unit. She had to lie about his being a relative, because the authorities had become exceedingly puritanical in such matters. Anyway, since she was Marion's sister, under the skin, it was not really a lie.

The officer was amenable, and by a wonderful stroke of luck she could live in her old room. In the frenzy of war preparation, the knowledge that every inch of living space would be needed, the gutted wing had been partially restored. And the nurses billeted in Elena's room had just been transferred to a field hospital south of the river. So she moved in with her nephew, and again found an old brown blanket to hang up. The boy knocked up some wood from a packing case to cover the shattered window; which made the room, in the depths of winter, terribly dark. They had only a candle. But through the slits of the packing case she could glimpse, to her joy, the maple. Its branches were black with soot, but it still lived, and seemed to stretch out its arms to greet her.

When they had been using the room for about a week, Elena had a strange and beautiful dream. It was anything but beautiful to start with: she was shaken awake by a guard and told to go to the interrogation room. She went along the corridor to the room in a kind of sleepwalk, wearing only her cotton nightdress. The interrogation room was bare except for two wooden chairs facing each other. An interrogator was standing in the corner, his back to her. She stood waiting in terror for him to turn round. Then she heard him say, 'My sister, Life!' and she recognized the title of one of Michael's earliest poems even before she recognized his voice. She spoke his name, tentatively, as he turned with a smile and stepped forward into the light. Wearing white trousers and a green open-necked shirt, he looked younger than when she had first known him. She started forward to embrace him but he took a step back, holding up his hand warningly, but still smiling, and gazing warmly into her eyes. 'Remember I'm dead!' he said with a chuckle.

He invited her to sit down in one of the chairs and he also sat. And then he told her things which came as a revelation to her. She discovered who she was, the purpose and meaning of her life, and that she need not fear, now or ever, 'the guest who calls by night'. (As a joke he was quoting one of his sister's lines that Elena had not yet heard.) Having told her these things, he said, 'Now you can go to the toilet.' Elena said she didn't need to, but Michael said, with a twinkle in his eye, 'Go anyway!'

When she woke, Elena remembered the whole dream vividly. Having used the bucket (naturally, the plumbing wasn't working), she stood on the lavatory seat and felt in the cistern. Her hand brought out one of those zip-up toilet bags that people used to be able to buy. Inside it she found, along with an old razor blade, a piece of paper with typing on it. It was obviously one of Michael's worksheets, but she couldn't begin to place it. Baffling as it was, it went into her memory, then back into the toilet bag and into the cistern.

She tried to persuade the boy to learn some of his relatives' work, but he was too young, too unwell still, and easily bored. There were other things he wanted to do, during the rare hours when his aunt was not on duty.

He was very fond of his new aunt. Just like his uncle's wife who had looked after him after his gran fell sick, she was pleasantly curved, tending to plumpness; but of course he had never got quite so close to his foster mother's body. Elena let him get really close. She was his first experience, his heart pounded as the time came nearer for her to come down from the ward. It was beautiful to rest his head against her jolly, plump breasts and to suck her nipples in the way she suggested. She would sometimes tease him, though! The first time she let him pull up her skirt, she gave him no help at all in dealing with those complicated, unfamiliar things she wore; she just lay back and smiled! How to go about dealing with such fascinating complications – the army bloomers with the elastic legs (just as well, with such poor heating), and under that – the strong suspenders fastened to the tops of the thick stockings ... What did you do with all this, when a woman just lay there and smiled?

They were amazing things, he decided – suspenders. He got his wristwatch tangled up in one of them when she lay asleep, and he was sure she would tick him off. The intricate way they unfastened and fastened, when she showed him, and the way they stretched out her stockings to breaking point – it was as if his bursting cock were throwing solid shadows of itself on to her thighs. And he liked the silky slithery feeling of her bloomers. He enjoyed lying in her lap and caressing their silkiness, with the elastic straps tight under that slipperiness, and the bump of the clips and buttons. And he loved the strange scent exuding from it all. She would throw her slip and skirt over his head, and let him lie there in the blackness, breathing it all in with his sharp nostrils.

Amazing, too, that when all those intriguing things were off, you just had to push against that pink hairy slit, with a little guidance from her hand, and you would glide in so moistly, so easily, so far! Up to the hilt! He had worried like mad about it, when the boys joked about it in school and in the barracks, but he needn't have worried.

In the endless hours when she was not there, while gunfire and shellfire sounded outside, he lay on the bed in the dark, recalling and longing, and there was a peculiar mixture of explosions and music and sinfulness and happiness going on inside him, and he would sniff his fingers to see if she was still there.

Elena knew she was doing the right thing. After all he had gone through – wasn't this healing and good? And either – or both – of them might die at any moment. She was sure her friends would understand. It was all the more health-giving for him in that she was not pretending; she really did enjoy it. She liked being a mother figure for a change! She liked pleasing him, not only in that way but in scrounging an egg from the hospital kitchen and cooking it for him on the primus. The sex was sweet; how refreshing was his innocence. How lucky she had not caught anything in that terrible brothel, how lucky she had always been. She felt a great affection for this boy, and that was blessedly new; and he was clean, and that was new too.

If, as she strongly suspected, he was her friends' son, he was a credit to them. The poetess had no need to feel such remorse. He appeared to have inherited all their best qualities. Except maybe their talent. That remained to be proven, and was hardly the most important thing.

Chapter Forty-Three

When they had 'made a desert and called it peace', the two sides wearily agreed to formalize the division of the city, by building a vast rampart, a kind of Great Wall of China, along no-man's-land, and to extend it until the entire country was split. The wall was policed by a neutral army, and both sides obviously also kept a watchful eye on things. In the city itself, the only break in the wall was where the river flowed through, but there are ways of policing even water. Brother was rent from brother, mother from son, husband from wife, lover from lover. More seriously, on one side there was no power station, and on the other side no gasometer. But generally, although there were occasional border incidents, the rampart served its purpose well enough.

The prison in which the poetess had been housed had fallen to the enemy quite early in the conflict. Following interrogation and internment, she had hunted everywhere for her son, thinking he too might have been captured; but to no avail. After the war, there was still no way of getting firm news of anyone. Her brother, of course, was quite well known, and some attempt had been made to find out his fate. There was evidence that he was alive, evidence that he was dead.

Maybe some day someone would defect and give her the truth. Of her son, and still less of Elena, a nonentity, there was no hope of ever hearing.

Marion herself had become something of a celebrity. Her early work was already well known, and there was great interest in artistic circles to read her later work. A Collected Poems had been published, she had been photographed, interviewed, paid large sums of money to do poetry readings. She ought to have been pleased with herself, but somehow it seemed not to matter – to be somehow phoney. She went on writing, and her new work was much admired; but the umbilical cord between her and her poems had been cut. Like an astronaut, she floated away from the mother ship, futile and gravityless. She longed for 'her' city to restore her, and in a way she was still in the city; but it was no longer hers. Reconstruction had made it unrecognizable. She hated these high, glass-and-concrete structures, that had no connection with the real world and no organic form. She lived in one herself, a beautiful apartment on the twentieth floor of a tower block belonging to the university. She had a professorship teaching Creative Writing. The apartment had everything she could need: wall-to-wall books, a plush three-piece suite, cocktail cabinet, kitchen unit, big ice box . . . The bathroom alone was bigger than the room she had shared with Elena and her brother. There was music or television at the touch of a button.

On this sunny July evening she looked out of the window and could see, through the gaps between apartment blocks, glimpses of the lagoon and the sea beyond. From a friend's apartment in a neighbouring block, she could look over the Wall and see the street where the house was, by the little canal. She had borrowed some very strong binoculars, and could even make out the house itself. It was something to know that it still stood. Around it there were many ruins; not much rebuilding had gone on yet on the other side, though there was a new bridge across the river and scaffolding around the cathedral dome.

From her own window, though, the only houses visible were a thousand other apartments like hers, in which people were drinking glasses of milk or orange juice, pulling off their ties and unbuttoning their shirts, mixing cocktails, switching on the tv for the news, making dinner, glancing through the evening paper . . .

The poetess had married again and divorced again. Mostly it had been her fault, she admitted. They had quarrelled over her un-willingness – her inability – to cope with having children. But also, at a deeper level, the marriage had foundered on just this emptiness that she felt, this blankness of freedom (for she could go anywhere and do anything), this urbanity and suavity; this not having anything to push against. She had even been happier living under the skylight with Elena and the Jewess; even though she had lately written of lying there and watching the full moon's 'O-gape of despair'.

She had to summon up the energy to go out. A nice man from the sociology department was taking her out to dinner at a new Italian restaurant that people spoke well of. They hadn't yet made love but perhaps he would want to tonight. After she had bathed she took out her cap from the bathroom cabinet, squatted down and put it in.

If they did go to bed, he would have to wear a condom too, and she wondered if he would bring one or if he would imagine she would resent it as a sign of presumption. She hated the thought of abortion, and she must not have a baby. Her thoughts went back on to the rails of her remorse, her inexpiable guilt, her grief. She had loved her son beyond measure (that was clear in her poems) but she could never cope with bringing him up. She tried to call up his face, but failed again. Loved faces always evaded her, whereas she had a clear picture of lesser friends.

She felt like wearing her new slacks, but they might not let her into the restaurant, so she chose the simple black frock. At the dress-ing table she brushed her long fair hair, checking the roots carefully, and put on a touch of lipstick. Everyone told her she was beautiful, as well as dedicated, talented, clever – and lucky. Even her name was a beautiful one for a poet, so they told her. She didn't think so. She did not like her name. It cleaved to every disaster, itself a disaster.

Returning to the lounge, she helped herself to a gin, and sipped while she painted her nails. When the polish was dry, she flipped through a boring magazine, and waited. The phone rang. It was her date, sounding nerve-strung and apologetic. He couldn't make it. His ex-wife had rung, hysterical, saying she had to get away on her own for a couple of days or she'd go mad, and would he please come round and look after his kids. Marion could hear one of the kids baw-ling in the background. He was sorry; he'd been so much looking forward to it. Perhaps at the weekend? Marion said, yes, certainly, if he was free, and he mustn't worry. She could come over and help him, she offered; but he said, thanks but no, she'd better not, the traffic was terrible tonight because of the ball game.

She changed into her housecoat and made herself a sandwich. While eating it she watched some television, an early-evening comedy show that touched upon love affairs and divorce, but scrupulously avoided any hint of truth; all the characters were sprinkled with icing sugar. The other channels were even worse; she flicked back to the comedy programme and found a soothing male voice using that lovely word 'tender', repeatedly, to characterize a particular company's toilet paper. She switched off, feeling dirtied, as she did when they showed violence, in the same bland way, on the news. Here the violence was to language, she was watching the death of language and the death of feeling. She was in at the kill.

She put a Bartók quartet on the gramophone, and decided to read again the book of translations of her brother's verse plays. It was difficult to assess how good or bad these versions were, because all the time she was hearing the original words, which were so much finer. She was coming to believe more and more that these two plays, so different, were the poles around which all the rest of her brother's work revolved: the first, *The Wedding Party*, unmatched in spiritual depth, the second, *Snow Queen*, unmatched in material breadth. Also, now that she was compelled, as it were, to read them together, she could see quite clearly that the heroine in each was one and the same woman – was Elena, in fact. (Even now she felt a brief pang of jealousy at this recognition.) There was also, in the comedy and the tragedy, a developing allegory in the central character: the innocent girl becoming the loving bride and mother, her love becoming tainted with corruption, and passing again into purity through the appearance of her daughter.

A smile touched her lips. In this version, the name of the bride's aunt, the good soul who 'gaily forgives' herself all her sins of the flesh, was simply transliterated. In the original it was an anagram of 'cunt-lips'. She wondered if she could get away with a reference to this in her review. Probably; they were very liberal. She noted that the translator made reference to her own conviction that the comedy was incomplete, and that a final scene existed, or once existed. She racked her brains yet again to hook out some remark her brother had made about it. But no, it was gone; she, with her excellent memory, to fail on such a vital point – it was tragic.

Reading his poetry always made her itch to be writing her own. But she forced herself to glance first through the assignment her students had handed in. With the promised reward of another gin and a cigarette when she had got through them (she was trying to cut down), she took the typescripts out of her briefcase. It was a mistake to read them after the two great plays. They depressed her again. With very few exceptions they lacked form and style and any sense of the beauty of words. Some of them couldn't even spell. They all said the same thing, in effect: 'I'm neurotic/frustrated/on drugs/the world is crazy/shit/a blank abyss of emptiness.' Christ, it was awful! What was she doing? They were so frank with their obscenities and the details of their sex lives, they obviously thought they were terribly bohemian; but for Marion their avoidance of grace and beauty and form made them seem drably puritan. She couldn't grade them in her present state; it would be unfair. She put the papers back in her case and poured a large gin.

And all these nice, mixed-up boys and girls were going around thinking they had written a masterpiece.

Dusk had fallen, and the geometric wilderness was lighting up. Old ladies were drinking their goodnight milk, and wondering why their sons hadn't phoned. Men with paunches were drinking root beer and watching the ball game. Their wives were planning who they could invite to dinner some night soon.

Chapter Forty-Four

She switched on the reading lamp, drew the curtains, poured herself another drink, and opened her notebook. Before she could bring herself to look at what she was working on, she lit a cigarette; a cigarette normally made it look better. Tonight it did not. What she had written struck her as banal, embarrassing, strained. She was not a poet at all, she had fooled everyone, she was incapable of putting two words together. She was as bad as the worst of her students.

The phone made her jump. She was relieved to be interrupted. But when she picked it up there was a click and the line went dead. The same thing happened twice more, over the next fifteen minutes. It scared her a little. There was a sex maniac on the loose. He was checking that she was in. He was probably already on his way up in the lift. She went to the outside door and made sure it was double locked. She put on some Mozart and returned to the poem, crossing through line after line, wincing that she could be so bad.

Her new lines were no better, and she scratched most of them out too, reinstating some of the old ones ('Go, child, who is my sin . . .' 'I'm no more your mother/Than the cloud . . .'). The fact that the poem was very personal increased her gloom. She had been driven to write like this for some time; personal and specific poems, detailing – as though to an analyst – the list of her crimes and the crimes she had suffered or witnessed. She had never before written so nakedly about her parents: that pure and terrible man who stared into hundreds of eyes each day but avoided his children's; that pallid, overwrought woman. And about her failed marriages and flawed affairs – why was she so good at friendship, so bad at love? She would also return, obsessively, to the things she had suffered and witnessed when in prison and, for a short while, in a mental institution. She had been so affected by some of the sights in the prison, and by other even more dreadful things she read and heard about after the war, that she had thought it impossible to write poetry at all, it seemed irrelevant. She could bear her own suffering, but not other people's: yet the suffering was endless. She had cracked up.

And there were the poems about her son ('my son, my terror'), the guilt she could never 'weep out' of putting him away into someone else's hands.

Her gloom and agitation grew. The hand shook that held the cigarette. The feeling was in control of the form, and that shouldn't be; there ought to be a kind of marriage.

She was no good as a woman, no good as a poet; and a failure as a teacher too. For wasn't this the sort of poetry her students, in their respect and reverence for her, were trying to imitate? The faults she was angry with were the faults she was teaching them!

She shut the notebook, threw it in a drawer, and paced about the room, drawing deeply on her cigarette. She tried to call a girlfriend to ask her round for a nightcap, but her friend was out.

She recognized all the signs of acute depression, and wondered what to do about it. One could do nothing. She felt wicked and untalented and lonely because she was wicked and untalented and alone. Pills didn't cure that. She was sweating; it was a sticky, close night and the air conditioning did not seem to be working properly. She took off her housecoat and her stockings, and lay on the sofa in her slip, feeling like the original slattern. She finished the bottle of gin. She lifted the magazine from the coffee table and found two coins there that she hadn't noticed before and didn't know where they came from. It struck her as a bad omen. 'I am saving these/coins for death,' she remembered.

She breathed more quickly and excitedly. She would make something out of this evening. As a carpenter makes a chair out of a shapeless block she would make her death. She went to the curtains and drew them back. Only a few lights still burned. The night was immense. Sheet lightning from over the gulf played greenishly between the blocks. A star fell, slowly, towards the airport. She went to the clothes closet and put on her raincoat. When she had buttoned it and tied the belt she took her donor card from her purse and pushed it in her pocket. She thought of any letters that might be embarrassing for the senders but could think of none. She returned to the lounge, switched off the lamp, and stood six feet from the window. The glass was strong, but would not resist an impact such as this. She drew in her breath and ran for the window, turning her body as she did so. She heard the crack of the impact and even as she rebounded from the glass (the architects were wise men) she felt herself crashing through into the cool air and beginning her wheeling flight down through the sky.

Chapter Forty-Five

Or perhaps she had been saved by Elena's dream, so long ago, of falling from a great height to her death? Perhaps that dream existed to permit her friend to live, as falling stars permit the flight of starlings, as the stillness of birches permits the racing of zebras.

The island cemetery in the lagoon, where Marion wished to be buried, because it was overgrown and abandoned to butterflies, remained undisturbed. But in those still, oppressive weeks, in the richer half of the city, many did fall. One, a woman, was watched by millions as she fell, no one knew why. Beautifully caught by a lucky cameraman (he had been filming a demonstration), and skilfully edited, with close-ups and slow motion, freezing her at different angles and postures against the many-windowed façade, her fall took on a thrilling balletic beauty. Tastefully the film cut back into long shot when she was upside down and indecent; tastefully it cut off as a streetlight came up into view below a gracefully outflung arm. Seen in the evening news, after the heavier items, it was dramatic and riveting. Only an office cleaner, not very bright, but when she fell a star was born.

Marion saw her fall. Curled up on her sociologist friend's sofa, she grew rigid, unable to blink. She lived the woman's death long after it was over; and wondered, again, how it was possible to go on breathing.

The tragic little film was 'borrowed' on the other side for the newsreels, to illustrate the suicidal despair of their imprisoned brothers and sisters, as if to say – be grateful for our health visitors with their polite hats and wonder cures. The evening Elena saw it she caused a scene by bursting into tears; and her sobs were so infectious that an old man sitting behind her took it up, and soon there wasn't a dry eye in the place. The crying carried on into the main film, a farce. If Elena's embarrassed companion hadn't hustled her out (her face a mess of wet mascara), and so allowed the audience to fight the virus off before they went out into the packed streets, there's no telling what might have happened ... A flood – who knows? – fish nuzzling the bronze eyes of the statue on the embankment – a tidal wave sweeping over the island of new immigrants in the harbour mouth, sweeping over the raised torch of the great figure of Love on the rock outside the gulf ... for they had bottled up their tears for so long, there seemed no end to how much they could cry.

Elena was too upset to explain that what had *really* made her burst into tears (for her mind had been straying and she'd thought a preview was being shown) was – not only the usual thing but ... suddenly and for no reason remembering a baby lying awake under the picture of a ship, and wondering what had happened to him.

Chapter Forty-Six

Cautiously boats laden with goods nosed past the Wall, in both directions; and the following Easter, passenger boats pushed through the melting ice, to allow a brief visit to relatives.

Marion visited the house simply as the best place to start searching, and was amazed and overjoyed to learn, from a man in the hallway, that Elena was living there – and in her old room too. The hugs, the kisses, the exclamations of wonder, can be imagined. When these emotional greetings had subsided just a little, Elena introduced her new husband. Marion shook his hand and peremptorily suggested he take a walk for an hour or two – she wanted to talk to her friend! Meekly he took his hat and went out. The poetess 'owned up' to being as imperious as ever, and hung her head for shame. Throwing their arms round each other, they went into gales of laughter, at the meek, surprised way he had taken his hat and left.

But in a moment there were tears, as Marion learnt that her brother was indeed dead; and tears, of happiness and relief, as she learnt that her 'nephew' was alive, and in the city. Elena ran to the telephone on the landing to ring him up and tell him the wonderful news. While they were waiting for him to visit, Elena sheepishly confessed to her brief affair with him, and said she had had some trouble sorting it out, as the lad had taken it far more seriously than she had anticipated. But he was fine now, and often visited with his girlfriend, a fellow engineering student at the technical college, very pleasant and attractive. Marion was too excited and tensed-up about the coming meeting to worry about little things like an affair. And the meeting went well. The young man was very pleased to see his aunt again. It was nice to have a blood relative living.

After the success of the Easter boat trips, letters (under strict censorship) were allowed to pass, and Elena and Marion kept in close touch. During the summer Elena wrote to say that she had kicked out her husband. They had not been compatible; he had cramped her enthusiasm and spontaneity: 'He did everything by the book – even *that*!!!' A few weeks later, Marion's petition to be allowed to reside in the east of the city was granted. She moved in with Elena.

Elena is working hard, training to be a teacher of infants. She would prefer to teach older children, but wryly agrees with her college interview assessment that she is not academic enough. But she likes the little ones, and is enjoying her training. She has also rediscovered a childhood skill – playing the flute. Two evenings a week she rehearses with the college orchestra. Life is hectic, because Marion has always been rather hopeless at cooking and doing the humdrum chores. Elena copes, though, as she always has done, and her friend does her bit by standing for hours in the queues for food. There are still the queues that never seem to move; but at least they are not outside the prisons.

Life is hectic – but also a little easier. The poetess has seen some of her work published on this side; she is asked to give poetry readings at the Theatre. What gives her most pleasure is that ordinary people recognize her in the street and stop her with a smile to say thank you. She doesn't know what they are thanking her for. 'The Witness' does not appear in her book; but it is circulating in typescripts and perhaps the people who stop to thank her have read these poems. Some of Michael's work, too, has been published, thanks initially to the grotesque 'Ode to Victory' his sister wrote for him. He has been posthumously pardoned; scholarly essays are written about him. In a monograph on her brother's work, Marion has taken great delight in observing that the high-ranking officials who tormented him have 'retired to rest in card indexes and lists of names (with garbled dates of birth and death) in studies of his work'. Sightseers visiting the house where he lived are unimpressed by the lavish apartments assigned to important officials at the present time. Instead, they tour the servants' rooms, saying her brother was here, or her brother was not here. 'All the rest is of no interest to them.'

It is a sign of the cautious thaw that her sly and witty observation was allowed to pass (with the omission of 'who tormented him'). But the two friends are still guarded. They keep their fingers crossed. Marion still gives Elena her poems, as they are written, to be learnt by heart.

There is one man who will be haunted by Michael until the day of his death, and perhaps beyond. The gay impresario, the one-armed choreographer – old and stooping now, no longer an impresario nor a choreographer, but decidedly still gay and one-armed – came along to their room one evening to pour out his guilt. Threatened with the execution of his boyfriend, it was he who had revealed to the authorities the contents of the pantomime scene. It took such courage for him to confess his sin that Marion and Elena have had to forgive him. Now, he comes to see them quite often, and is relaxed enough to have a little pry into their business. 'What exactly *is* your relationship?' he will chuckle.

Elena, in her sprightly, teasing fashion, changes the subject. She well knows that all their friends are curious. Put to the rack of confession, Elena would no doubt disappoint them by saying that she had never been to bed with her friend 'in the fullest sense'. But they are extremely close, sharing meals, jokes, thoughts, tights, earrings, memories ... They are enjoying their respite from men. They believe that men have been responsible for most of the miseries in the world.

But they are far from disliking men or withdrawing into themselves. Elena's horizons are wider than they have ever been; and Marion, as ever, reconciles her jealously guarded privacy with an incomparable gift for friendship. Serious, grave, austere, for much of the time, regal even, with the conscious dignity of her art which is the *stélé* of too many nameless deaths; yet she can still make her friends fall off their chairs with laughter. Nor must you think they walk along with their eyes directed at the pavement. Their eyes still sparkle, and respond – though carefully. Marion particularly, with her fame and her dark, slanting, rather oriental eyes, is often troubled, as well as flattered, by the havoc she can unintentionally create. (Isn't there something of her, too, in the heroines of *The Wedding Party* and *Snow Queen?*) And Elena, though she dashes about much of the time in old jeans and sweater that the toddlers' grubby hands can't hurt, and rarely has time to put on any make-up in the mornings, gets more than her share of looks. Only last week, on the canal bus, she was approached by one of those men who are always on the lookout for attractive young women, and asked if she would like to earn a bit of spare cash posing for pin-up photos.

And talking of photos – Elena's picture has appeared on television. Peter's wife phoned her to tell her about it one night – mainly to satisfy her own curiosity. Mysteriously the photo of Elena and the child, on the poster extolling motherhood, had surfaced, and it had been used as a visual to a news item, the announcement of cash benefits for large families (the Pill, and easy abortions, have been cutting down the number of births rather alarmingly).

Peter and his new wife, whom he has never seen, come visiting quite a lot; and on Sundays, in summer, the young women stroll out along the river to have a glass of wine with them in the little, scruffy embankment café. He's as cheerful and extrovert as ever, and they have given him a small disability pension, which keeps body and soul together. Some of his paintings of Elena have fetched ridiculous prices, but he hasn't seen a penny of it. He doesn't worry; he's happy so long as he can keep working, in his new style that doesn't require eyes. Elena is not sure if it is 'art' exactly, but many of her friends think it's excellent. As with poems, she only 'knows what she likes' and feels ashamed of her ignorance. Whether the work is good or bad, the great thing, as she says, is that he's still painting. There is the possibility of an operation which might restore his sight. That would be wonderful, and they are keeping their fingers crossed.

One Sunday at the café, they bumped into a very old friend of Elena's, someone she hadn't seen for years: the sculptor, white-bearded now. He had been 'away', but had been pardoned, and was now hopeful of settling down again to his art, if he could re-learn his craft. He was very worried about that – would it still be 'there'? Elena offered to model for him when he had found himself a studio, and eventually he got to work on her. But she thinks that possibly his experiences have 'touched' him, somewhat, for when he invited her to look at what he'd done, he had made her body full of holes! There were holes where her breasts should have been! What was the use, she thought, of sculpting to a shapely body – and she knew without false modesty that hers *was* shapely still – if you didn't make the most of it? Holes were great, but only in the proper places!

So their life continues – happy compared with what it *has* been, even though in too many ways nothing has changed. The wealthy officials are back in their ample apartments, and have their weekend retreats too; there are still the special shops catering to their every whim, while the ordinary people queue for three hours for a couple of oranges. It is still 'the people's this' and 'the people's that', driving *people* (who have next to nothing) mad to distraction.

And many of the changes that have taken place seem, to Elena and Marion, changes for the worse. Too many huge, ugly apartment blocks have gone up, just as on the other side. On the site of the old ghetto, a vulgar Olympic stadium has been erected. Most of the churches have been demolished, and the others stay locked. This grieves them both. Elena isn't overtly religious, but she believes in God. She has found another silver crucifix to replace the one that was stolen from her on the night of her arrest; and she prays before she goes to sleep, when she remembers to.

The Wall remains, an eyesore, an affront to decency, and is likely to stay for years to come. Jealousy abounds. The authorities in the east, for example, knowing that they can't catch up in other respects, have rebuilt the cathedral as an observatory. That splendid white dome now has a slit running over its top, through which one of the world's most powerful telescopes searches the sky. The university observatory, west of the Wall, is a midget by comparison! But at least, there is pleasure that the ancient dome has been restored, even in its new form. The poetess even finds it moving – religious, in its way – as a recent poem tries to express ('I am a singing cupola,/Rounded and mysterious as a hull . . .'). She has reverted to her restrained impersonal style, and is at peace with it.

She is happy, too, about her son. One day she told him the whole story. He is rather proud of his mother, and she of him; he has just graduated in engineering. But they both know they would never get on if they lived together. Fortunately there is no need. He is about to get married, and has been allotted a two-room apartment.

Usually when he visits his mother he finds another man already there: a man with a black beard who looks older than he actually is. The serious and courteous young engineer is not put out; far from it, for this man is the nearest to a father that he has ever known.

About six months ago, Marion had a telegram which made her legs turn to jelly. It was from her brother Joseph. He was on his way to see them. Three days later he arrived. Underneath his beard, Elena could see how much he resembled his younger brother. He had not been shot – that was just another of the million false reports – simply sent to one of the worst camps for an indeterminate period and without right of correspondence. During the war he had been released to serve in a penal battalion whose task it was to clear minefields. He had been captured but managed to escape and return to his own lines. He had been sent back to the camp as an enemy spy. Now they had pardoned him. Such things often happened.

He was amazed – delighted – when Elena came out with one of his poems that she did not understand. He gets on with her like a house on fire, as if he has known her all his life. Sometimes he looks at her in a special way, and she blushes, but it is too simple to say that he desires her. She reminds him of his beautiful young wife whose death had broken his heart – but also of the daughter he has always wanted, the daughter who perished in her mother's womb at the time of the tragic accident.

He visits them so often he might just as well move in – and is thinking of doing just that. Elena and Marion are learning his poems of camp life, that are still too dangerous to write down. They are like chips of radioactive granite. It is a good thing that in the occasional street searches the police don't use Geiger counters!

Tonight – it is a warm white night in June – brother and sister are out reading poems to some of the young people with whom they get on so well. Elena is quite pleased to have some privacy. She is sitting by the window playing her flute and conversing with the maple. I too am glad of the chance to talk to her alone. Finding the door unlocked I have crept in. She senses someone is in the room, puts down the flute on the window ledge, and turns. Whether she is annoyed or not, she gives me that sunny smile and, pleased or embarrassed, it is hard to tell which, pushes her hair back from her eyes.

Ian McEwan
The Cement Garden £1.25

'In many ways a shocking book, morbid, full of repellant imagery – and irresistibly readable . . . the effect achieved by McEwan's quiet, precise and sensuous touch is that of magic realism' NEW YORK REVIEW OF BOOKS

'A little masterpiece of appalling fascination' DAILY MAIL

'For a first novel, it is a darkly impressive piece of work . . . a touch of real fictional genius' THE TIMES

Bruno Schulz
The Street of Crocodiles £1.25

When Bruno Schulz was murdered by the Nazis in 1942 he had published only two works of fiction, *The Street of Crocodiles* being the first – a startling blend of the real and the fantastic in a collection of stories evoking the author's strange boyhood in a provincial Polish town and the characters – particularly his father: textile merchant and incorrigible fantasist – of the neighbourhood. This book brings to light a strange neglected genius.

'One of the great writers' JOHN UPDIKE

Josef Skvorecky
The Bass Saxophone £1.25

Two novellas by the distinguished Czech exile which evoke with poignant irony and dark fantasy the everyday life lived under totalitarianism – whether Nazi or Communist.

Skvorecky introduces the stories with a brilliant personal memoir of jazz, in Czechoslovakia a persistent and enduring voice of freedom under two tyrannies. A triumphant celebration of the beleaguered individual's resistance to drab uniformity and spiritual meanness.

'Gave me enormous pleasure . . . of all Skvorecky's remarkable works, these two are my favourites' GRAHAM GREENE

Aragon
Paris Peasant £1.50

One of the great works of surrealistic prose, containing the very kernel of surrealism: that the tangible world conceals marvels that only await revelation. Aragon seeks to capture this 'mythology of the modern' in his remarkable book.

A guided tour of out-of-the-way spots in Paris of the 1920s, the novel uses every resource of language to jolt the reader towards new values. Flights of lyricism, surges of aggression and sarcasm, humour and reflectiveness – a kaleidoscope of voices makes this a masterpiece of surrealism transcending the movement which inspired it.

'Fresh and alive . . . bold and aggressive . . . enduring charm and poetry' FINANCIAL TIMES

'Records and celebrates the mysteries of modern Paris' CAMBRIDGE REVIEW

B. Wongar
The Track to Bralgu £1

In these compelling stories B. Wongar examines the clash of cultures in Australia, and what it means to be a black man in a white man's continent.

With deep and savage irony, the whites' passion for uranium is juxtaposed with the near-extinction of so many Aborigine tribes. As holy caves and tribal places disappear, Wongar's characters call on the spirits of rain and wind, but even Jambwal the Thunder Man cannot drive the miners away. Though the struggle be bitter, the track to Bralgu leads ahead, to the ancestors' spirits, transmuted as bird and star and tree, awaiting rebirth . . .

'The finest poetry composed on the continent of Australia are the ancient incantatory songs of the aboriginal peoples . . . Mr Wongar's arresting chants do full honour to that tradition' THOMAS KENEALLY, NEW YORK TIMES

Robert Hunter
The Greenpeace Chronicle £2.50

It began in Vancouver in 1971. As the USA stood ready to detonate an atomic explosion on the Aleutian island of Amchitka, a handful of radicals aboard an eighty-foot fishing boat set course for the testing zone. Greenpeace was born.

Robert Hunter chronicles the next seven years, a desperate courageous and inspired attempt to stem the tide of destruction on this planet. The story of fighters against the nuclear armourers, the whalers, the seal hunters . . . face to face with the full ecological horrors of our century.

Hunter S. Thompson
The Great Shark Hunt £2.95

strange tales from a strange time

Here is the first British publication of the best of Gonzo in one chunky volume. From Private Thompson in trouble with the air force, to a devastating portrait of the ageing Muhammed Ali – taking in the Kentucky Derby, Nixon in '68, McGovern in '72, Fear and Loathing at Watergate, Jimmy Carter: a compendium of decadence, depravity and horse sense.

'No other reporter reveals how much we have to fear and loathe, yet does it so hilariously' CHICAGO TRIBUNE

'. . . a streaker at Queen Victoria's funeral'
NEW YORK TIMES BOOK REVIEW

You can buy these and other Picador books from booksellers and newsagents; or direct from the following address:
Pan Books, Sales Office, Cavaye Place, London SW10 9PG
Send purchase price plus 20p for the first book and 10p for each additional book, to allow for postage and packing
Prices quoted are applicable in the UK

While every effort is made to keep prices low, it is sometimes necessary to increase prices at short notice. Pan Books reserve the right to show on covers and charge new retail prices which may differ from those advertised in the text or elsewhere